DARLING DUNCAN

GEORGIA PEACHES, BOOK 3

VANESSA GRAY BARTAL

DRY CREEK PRESS

*D*uncan Shepherd was tired. *That should be my epitaph,* he thought, staring listlessly at the wall while his baby, Darla, slept in his arms. Tired was a state of being now, ever since Darla's birth. Finding rest had become his number one goal in life. He had no energy for anything else, only sleep. Sleep was life now.

His best friend, Sterling, let himself in the front door and sat on Duncan's couch. Duncan shoved Darla at him without remorse. What was the point of having a best friend if not to get him to do stuff for you? Besides, Sterling loved holding the baby, was a self-avowed baby addict.

"There's this fat girl at the gym," Duncan said, apropos of nothing.

"All the best romances start with those words," Sterling said, staring hard at Darla's face, scanning it for changes. Duncan recognized the expression because he did the same thing daily. She was changing so fast; it broke his heart a little.

"No, see, that's the thing. I was thinking about asking her if she'd be my nanny, but I don't want her to think I'm hitting on her. Because, as I mentioned, she's fat and I'm, well, you know." He motioned to his face, his beautiful, glorious face.

"I'm confused about my part in this conversation," Sterling said.

"You're good at this sort of thing, at being nice to women. How can I ask her about a nanny job without making her think I'm hitting on her? The one thing I don't need right now is another addition to my fan club."

"Open your mouth. Make sure and talk a lot, and it won't be a problem. Trust me, say a few words, let her see the real you, and she will not be interested," Sterling said.

Duncan gave a nod. "Right, thanks." He rested his head on the couch behind him, already in sleep mode, when Sterling spoke again.

"So Alby and I are engaged."

Duncan sat up, facing him. "What? When did that happen?"

"Last night."

"How could you not have told me?" Duncan demanded.

"I don't know. It's all about you, after all," Sterling said.

"But we tell each other everything," Duncan protested. He hated being kept out of the loop on Sterling's life, loathed it. It made him feel insecure, like his foundation was shifting.

"Not about Alby, we don't," Sterling said.

"I've known her as long as you have," Duncan pouted.

"She's going to be my wife. I'm not telling you personal details about my wife, as I have told you many, many, a hundred thousand times. When you decide to settle down, you'll understand. It's not the same."

"I don't like that," Duncan declared. He reached for Darla, but Sterling held her possessively away.

"Don't be ugly," Sterling admonished.

"I wouldn't begin to know how," Duncan said. "Am I allowed to know when you're getting hitched, or is that top secret, too?"

"Of course you're allowed to know. You're my best man."

Duncan blinked, a bit overwhelmed. Of course he would be Sterling's best man. Who else did they have but each other? But the past year of their relationship had been tricky, fraught with ups and downs and an almost split. It meant a lot to know he was still Sterling's person; it meant everything. "Well, good," he said at last, blinking hard.

"I also thought I should prep you because Birdie's coming home for it."

"Of course she is," Duncan said. He aimed for nonchalance and failed mightily. Birdie. Coming home after a year's absence. Previously he thought he would die because of her absence. Now he thought he might die because of her return. He wasn't ready to face her again, wasn't ready at all.

"Are you breathing?" Sterling asked.

No, he was not. He sucked a deep breath, expanding his chest as far as it would go. "Is *he* coming with her?"

"You really think he'd let her come back here alone? To you?"

Duncan grinned at that. Birdie might not be his in the most technical sense, but he was stiff competition for her current boyfriend, Hayden Paxton. The stiffest, in fact. Because he knew something about Birdie no one else did: she was in love with him. Sure, she might say she loved Hayden, might even feel it a bit for the only guy besides Duncan who had ever paid her any attention. But she loved him, too. He was sure of it, as sure as he had ever been of anything. And next time she was home, things would be different. *He* would be different. He would show her a new Duncan, a better one.

"You're staring dreamily into space," Sterling noted.

"I was thinking fondly of sleep," Duncan lied.

"Go find some. I've got this peanut," Sterling said, leaning close to press a kiss to Darla's forehead. She flinched but otherwise didn't stir.

Duncan didn't have to be told twice. He propped his feet on the coffee table and fell into a coma, not bothered at all by Sterling's continued presence at his side. In fact he found it comforting. If there was one thing he hated, it was being alone.

CHAPTER 2

*H*e was staring at her again. For the fifth time in two weeks, Marlow happened to be at the gym at the same time as the gorgeous guy. And, as before, he kept darting her looks. She wasn't certain if the looks were supposed to be sultry or if he was so ridiculously good looking he couldn't help but smolder. Whatever the case, he was giving her the creeps. He was much too exquisite to be at the gym by himself this late on a weeknight; ergo, he must be a serial killer. She racked her weight and his eyes flicked to her again. Yep, definite Ted Bundy vibes.

One other person was in the gym, one person who now stood between her and certain dismemberment. Her murderer-to-be was probably a cannibal. That was probably why he'd selected her for his next victim because, unlike all the rangy thin girls, she had enough fat on her thighs to make them tasty. The non-murderer was wrapping it up and preparing to leave. That meant Marlow had to leave, too. No way would she be stuck alone in an all-night gym with the Charles Manson acolyte.

She'd only been at the gym for twenty minutes, but no matter. Better to remain chubby than wake up dead tomorrow. She cleaned the weights, tossed her towel in the bin, and followed the non-murderer outside. And then immediately realized she'd left her keys inside. With Jack the Ripper.

Was it worth it? Could she walk home? Yes, but then she wouldn't be able to get inside the door when she reached it. Maybe she could sneak in and out before he noticed.

No such luck, though. As soon as she slipped in the door, he glanced up, eyes lighting with a weird sort of satisfaction. *He's going to make puppets from my skin,* Marlow thought, forcing her eyes away. She strode to the back, grabbed her keys, and positioned them like little daggers between her fingers.

She began to think she might make it back out the door when he spoke. "Hey," he said, tone friendly and innocuous.

No, thanks, Jeffrey Dahmer. I'm not buying any today.

She pushed through the door and picked up her pace, doing a fast trot to her car. He pushed open the door and followed. "Wait up," he called.

She started to sprint.

He sprinted behind her. "Hey, I just want to talk to you."

With chloroform, I bet.

She didn't pause until she reached her car. And then she dropped her keys. She bent to pick them up but couldn't find them. And then he was there, her personal Freddy Kruger. It was like every horror story she'd ever watched as she stared at his shoes and contemplated how best to get away.

Slowly, she levered herself up, pressed against her car. When she was fully upright, she sprang away, sprinting in the opposite direction of the psycho.

"Hey," he said, sounding annoyed now. And he was chasing her, further proving his desperation to roast her leg bones over a spit with salted potatoes. Probably a salad, too. He looked the sort who would feel it necessary to add vegetables to every meal.

She had no idea where she was going, but it didn't matter because he easily overtook her, tackling her as soon as they reached the grass at the edge of the parking lot. *A grassy knoll; I'm going out like Kennedy,* she thought, and then he was on her and they were tussling, grunting as they wrestled back and forth. At one point she thought she had him, and then he put her in some kind of wrestling hold and pinned her beneath him, panting as he stared down at her.

"Don't eat me," she pled. "I'm all gristle."

His eyes narrowed in confusion. "What? I just wanted to ask you a question."

She paused. "You chased me through a parking lot and tackled me to ask me a question?"

"I guess it triggered my predatory instincts. Like a dog."

Whimpering now, she began squirming to get away.

"Geez, you're strong," he said, banging her wrists into the ground as he applied more weight to keep her still.

"Haven't the others fought to get away?" she asked, panting.

"Getting away is usually the last thing on a woman's mind when I'm this close to them," he said, and then he winked.

Marlow turned her head back and forth, searching for the hidden cameras. Either he wasn't talking to her or he was putting on some kind of performance. "Are you for real?"

"I'm trying to have a conversation," he said.

"As it seems I have no other choice, go right ahead and ask your question, crazytown," she said.

"Are you over eighteen?"

She brought her feet up and tried to kick him off.

"No, wait, that came out wrong. It's just that you look young and I wanted to make sure…I need a babysitter."

A babysitter? He couldn't be that much older than her. "I'm not into that kind of thing, you perv," she said, twisting to get free once more.

"Would you just," he began and then put his full weight on her, squeezing out her air. "I have a baby and I am looking for a nanny. Until this moment you seemed halfway sane, so I thought I would give it a try."

She blinked at him. "You have a baby?"

He nodded.

"Where is she?"

"I set some cereal on the floor and left her at home. She's fine."

She began squirming again.

He sighed. "You seem to be lacking a sense of humor about my sanity. She's with her mother."

She stopped squirming and scowled. "Why do you say it like that? Did you buy her from a surrogate or something?"

"No, she was the product of a mistaken drunk hookup."

"So you're, like, the originator of old school romance, huh?" she said and was rewarded when he smiled. Except not really because he had that sort of smile that stuns, like one of those snakes that spits venom to paralyze prey. Marlow was frozen the same way, counting his teeth. He seemed to have more of them than other humans, and they gleamed supernaturally. "Do you use charcoal powder?"

"What?" he asked, confused.

"Those teeth, my lands. How do you get them that white?" She was glad he had her arms pinned because she was suddenly tempted to reach out and touch his incisors, like when you saw a knife and felt compelled to see if it was actually sharp. She wanted to watch him chew something, a carrot stick maybe. He could be one of those people with a weird YouTube channel, one where people watch his perfect teeth do things, smile, eat, mouth words.

"You're very odd," he declared.

"Says the man who has been pressed on top of me for the last ten minutes."

"It's strangely comfy here, kind of squishy," he noted, wriggling.

"You're not supposed to tell squishy people they're squishy. Does a woman have to be drunk to be with you? Otherwise I'm not seeing the appeal," she said.

"Why are women so huffy about their bodies? All I meant was that it's more comfortable to lay on you than, say, the cold, hard ground."

"Oh, swoon. It's like the poetry tumbles from your lips. Pro tip: you'd better thank the Good Lord every night you're pretty because, I'm here to tell you, it's all you've got."

He laughed and rolled off her, sitting up. "Believe it or not, I do all right."

"Yes, well, desperation does strange things to a person," she said, straightening her shirt. She felt oddly chilled without his warmth, which was weird because it was Georgia and ninety degrees at ten at night.

"No, this is good, this whole defensive banter thing. It would not do at all to have my nanny fall in love with me. This isn't a Lifetime movie."

"See, our minds were going in opposite directions. I was thinking more along the lines of *The Hand that Rocks the Cradle*."

He ignored her as if she hadn't spoken. "All I want is someone responsible and caring to watch my daughter. I travel a fair bit for my job, and I need to know she's in capable hands."

"How much does it pay?" she asked.

"Money grubbing, aren't you?" he said, tossing her a sideways glance.

"I'm greedy enough to want to be able to live on what I make."

"Twenty three thousand, but it includes room and board."

"You want me to live with you?" she asked, suspicious all over again.

"Do you not understand the definition of the word nanny? The baby's mom and I have agreed to share you."

She put her hands over her ears.

He took them away. "Not like that. Who made you this way? All I meant was that we like the continuity of having one sitter, so she'll bring the baby to my house during the days she has her and has to work, and you'll watch her for my days. And then sometimes I have to travel, so you'll be there for that, too."

"What about cooking and cleaning?" she asked.

"Can you cook?"

"Yes."

"If you cook, I'll pay you extra. I'm pretty tidy, so clean up after yourself and the baby."

"How do you have so much money?" she asked.

"I tackle women in parking lots and sell them on the black market," he said.

"Why didn't I make the cut?" she asked.

"You talk too much," he said. "And I'm a pharmaceutical rep, a really, really good one."

"What kind of house do you have?" she asked.

"Gingerbread. With all the trimmings."

"You're delusional if you think bringing a fat girl there is going to work out well for you," she said.

He laughed and swiped his hand over his face. "I have a big, rambling farmhouse, lots of room. And you'd have your own bathroom."

"How old is your daughter?"

"Ah, thank you for finally getting to the human element. Your character is shining really well right now. She's five months." He tipped his head at her. "You do have experience with children, right?"

"That's an odd thing to assume about someone. Do you think all chubby girls love kids?"

"Yes," he said.

"Well, you're probably right. As a group, we're jolly and naturally nurturing. Unless that kid is reaching for our private candy stash, and then look out." She smashed her fist into her open palm, and he laughed again.

"There might be something seriously wrong with you," he said.

"Drunken-hookup-glowing-teeth says what?" she replied.

He laughed again, pressing his hand to his eyes. "This is what my life has become. Are you interested in the job or not?"

"One condition," she said.

He dropped his hand from his eyes and regarded her warily.

She raised a finger and pointed it at him in warning. "Do not fall in love with me."

He expelled a puff of laughter and stuck out his hand to shake. "Deal."

CHAPTER 3

She was really quite pretty, for a fat girl. Beautiful, even. Not that Duncan was in the market. But he did have an eye for quality, for attractiveness. It was pleasant to think his daughter's caregiver would fit the bill and be nice looking. Completely insane, but not bad to look at, not bad at all. And she wasn't crazy in a harmful, dangerous way. It was more like, well, it was a lot like how Birdie was crazy, as if set apart from birth to be quirky and different. And maybe it was that comparison to Birdie that made Marlow endearing. Whatever the reason, he felt the arrangement would work out well, hopefully for both of them. Even Chelsea liked her, which was saying something because Chelsea didn't like anyone. The bad thing about having a baby, the *only* bad thing, as far as Duncan could tell, was that the baby's mother was such an unlikeable human being. It would be up to him to make sure Darla didn't turn out the same. Though how to enforce that was anybody's guess. "Don't turn out like your horrible mother," seemed the wrong thing to say to a child.

Maybe he could prevent it by virtue of being a good dad. Didn't girls need good dads to turn out well? He wondered if that was what went wrong with Chelsea. Maybe her dad was terrible. Duncan had no idea. He had never asked and had zero desire to know her more than he already did, which was to say not at all. Who she was or what she did had no impact on him, as long as it had no impact on Darla. It concerned him a bit that she might one day start dating again, might bring another man into Darla's life. He wasn't threatened, mind. He would always be Darla's dad. How could anyone top that? But knowing how horrible Chelsea was made him nervous she would drag some similarly horrible man into her midst and *that* would be a problem. No way would he let some reject from the loser pile near his daughter.

But, seeing as how Chelsea was as gobsmacked by parenthood as he was, he didn't see her dating anytime soon. The one thing he knew about her was that she was as tired as he was. When it was his turn with the baby, she slept, just like he slept when it was her turn. Single parenthood was not for the faint of heart, this much he knew for certain.

"So, you bought a giant farmhouse in the middle of nowhere," Marlow said at first sight of his house, a box of her things in tow. "Does it have a padded cellar to block the sounds of your victims' screams?"

"You're kind of obsessed with murder," he noted.

"Now you're catching on, Ace," she said, making a little shooting motion with her hand.

"Not that I owe you any explanation, being as how you're now officially my employee, but this was my grandparents' place, my family's ancestral farmhouse. I bought it from them last year."

"Who beat you with the sentimentality stick?"

"They needed an out, didn't want to sell to strangers," he said, shrugging. Plus he'd bought it for Birdie, intending it to be *their* ancestral home.

"Now *that* is attractive," she said, looking around the farm with fresh eyes.

"It needs some work," he said, feeling strangely self-conscious at her inspection. The farm was dated and in desperate need of renovation. He'd had big plans when he bought it. Then things didn't work out the way he intended with Birdie. Then he became a father. Now the task felt overwhelming. Maybe someday when he wasn't in survival mode he'd get back to it.

"No, it's great, really. It has a lot of charm," Marlow said sincerely, smiling as she scanned the vast space.

"You're not, like, falling in love with me now that you've seen my amazing house, are you?" he asked, only half joking.

"No, but I'm falling in love with the house," she said, shifting the box in her hands. "Should I select a room, or would you prefer me to get a hernia right here?"

"C'mon," he said, motioning with his head for her to follow him up the stairs. "My room, Darla's room, you. She's between us."

Instead of following him into her room, she paused on the threshold of Darla's room and flipped on the light. He wondered what she saw when she made her inspection, but "Hmm" was all she said.

He should probably help her unload her stuff. It was what a gentleman would do. It was what Sterling would do. Instead he sat on the couch with his feet up, watching curiously as she made trip after trip past him. Finally, she seemed to be done, a hard, hourglass case slung over her back.

"Guitar?" he guessed.

"Baby giraffe," she corrected. "My service animal, but he needs to be contained." She tapped the case.

"Should I always expect this level of sarcasm from you?" he asked, but he didn't really mind. At least she wasn't boring, which put her ahead of ninety percent of the women he knew.

"No, sometimes I'll *try* to be sarcastic, and then I'll make you cry using only the power of my words," she said, and then she closed herself in her room. He could hear her shuffling around up there, moving things, opening and closing drawers. The baby was with Chelsea. Sterling and Alby were doing whatever couples do together that doesn't require a third wheel. Duncan scanned the living room, tapped his foot a few times, then got up and darted up the stairs, pausing outside Marlow's door. He knocked. The sound came to a standstill.

"Yes?"

"What are you doing?"

"Unpacking."

"Why are you doing it with your door closed?"

"Because I didn't realize you were a voyeur," she said.

"Pretty sure that was implied in your contract. You're not going to be one of those weirdos who closets yourself in your room all the time, are you?"

She yanked open the door and startled at his nearness. "Do you want to tell me what this is about?"

"I have a low boredom threshold. It's practically a disability. I could probably get a prescription," he said, resting his shoulder on the jamb.

"Could you maybe cut to the chase and drop the odd subtext? What exactly do you want from me, in layman's terms?"

"Amuse me, monkey," he said, clapping his hands together a couple of times.

She regarded him a few beats in silence, then turned and faced her room. "Come in, I guess. You can watch me arrange my room. Currently I'm torn between putting my shirts in the middle or last drawer. It's fascinating."

Instead of taking the chair at her desk like a normal human would have, he lay sideways across her bed, the one she had only made five minutes ago with fresh sheets. "Tell me about you. What pertinent information should I know about my new nanny?"

"There's not a lot to tell. After my last prison stint, I swore I was going to get clean. And I have, mostly."

"Are you a local?"

"To this state, yes. To this town, no. I moved here a few months ago with my parents."

"Why?" he asked, resting his face in his hand.

"My dad's job."

"No, I mean why did you come with them? You're, what, twenty seven, twenty eight?"

"Twenty five," she said, irked that he'd overestimated.

He smiled, enjoying her annoyance. "Still a grownup in all the ways that count. Why did you move with your mommy and daddy?"

"It was a financial necessity. I've been waiting tables until I can get my career going," she said.

"What career is that? And if you say nanny, I'm going to start to believe in kismet."

"Swimsuit model," she said.

He squinted at her.

She tossed a wadded shirt at him. "You don't have to be *that* skeptical. Clearly I was joking."

He didn't say what he was thinking, that she could be a plus sized model. She was extraordinarily pretty, and her body wasn't grotesque. She was overweight but not enough to be shapeless. And she was tall. From his vantage point, she checked all the appropriate boxes for an oversized model.

"What about you? Has selling drugs always been your career ambition? Were you a high-school pusher turned pro?" she asked.

"I've always been particularly skilled at making people do things they don't want to do." He paused while she pretended to retch. "I always sort of figured sales would be my calling. Selling specialized pharmaceuticals is one of the more lucrative avenues."

"What does that mean, specialized pharmaceuticals?" she asked.

"Biologic, drugs derived from living cells."

"So you do actually sell humans," she noted.

He grinned at her. "Sometimes primates, depending on the drug. Either way, I make a boatload of money." Last year he'd made a hundred and thirty thousand; this year he was on track to make even more.

"That reminds me, I demand a raise," she said.

"Let's see you do some actual work first," he said.

"Do you want me to babysit a pretend baby to earn my keep?" she asked, somewhat absently. Her attention was on the clothes she was currently arranging in her drawer.

"You're doing it wrong," Duncan said.

She gaped at him. "How can I be doing it wrong when they're my clothes in my drawer?"

"Technically the drawer is mine, but you're supposed to turn them sideways so you can see everything at a glance. Did Marie Kondo teach you nothing?"

She reached out and touched the hem of his pants. "You do not spark joy. Away with you."

He kicked her hand away. "I'm just saying that if there's a right way and a wrong way, don't you always want to do it the right way?"

"How about I'll start taking life advice from you when you stop impregnating strangers," she said, stuffing a few more shirts the wrong way into her drawer.

"In my defense, she was not a stranger. She was my best friend's girlfriend."

"See, that makes me think you don't know the meaning of defense," she said. "I take it you and the friend are no longer friends and that is why someone who looks like you is hanging out with his nanny and taking note of her drawer arrangement."

"No, Sterling and I are lifers. There's no breaking up our duo."

"Then where is he at this moment?"

"With his girl. They're getting married." He shifted, resting his chin on his fist. She paused to toss him an exaggerated pout.

"Uh-oh, someone has the sads that his bestie is moving on."

"He's not moving on. I like Alby, too. We all went to school together. But they're in that phase, you know. The one where they still like each other. I'll swoop back in when they're ready to blow each other's brains out over which way the flap goes on the toilet paper."

"Something tells me you're nearby a lot when people are ready to blow someone's brains out," she said.

"Nah, I'm well loved," he said, aiming for meekness and failing completely.

She shook her head. "That is it, I am covering up that magic mirror."

He laughed and tossed back the t-shirt she had earlier tossed at him. "Something tells me I'm going to need every ounce of self-love to deflect your barbs."

"Fair point," she agreed.

"What do you do when you actually dislike someone?" he asked.

"I get quiet."

He gave an exaggerated shudder. "I can't imagine."

"What about you? What do you do when you're upset?"

"I start thinking about things," he said, giving a real shudder. There was nothing he loathed more than introspection.

"Having a baby didn't make you think about things?" she asked, turning to study him again.

"What's to think about? It's a done deal. How will pondering help? I'm being the best dad I know how, trying to co-parent with her heinous mother, even though she's the human version of a toothache. Why does it require more thought on my part?"

"Huh. So this whole shallow, self-involved thing you've got going on, it's really not an act?"

"No. I'm fairly amazing and my life is perfectly in order."

"Huh. So really all you want from me is to care for your daughter and keep you entertained?"

He smiled, relieved she finally understood. "What more is there?"

CHAPTER 4

*D*uncan was quickly becoming the most fascinating person Marlow had ever met. She had never encountered someone so unapologetically self-centered and shallow before. He seemingly did nothing unless it was for his benefit.

It was nothing to her, of course. His shallowness had no effect on her life. He was her boss, but it didn't feel like it. If he hadn't efficiently set up autopay into her bank account, she might forget entirely, might see him as merely a roommate.

They had two days to settle in and get acquainted, two days where she watched him, blatantly staring as she catalogued his ever-increasing superficiality. He served himself breakfast without pointing Marlow toward the cereal, finished the last of the milk without a word, took up all the spaces on the couch so she was forced to squish in the uncomfortable side chair, arranged his body so his stinky socks were directly in her face, blared his music when he woke at five in the morning, literally knocking her out of bed with fright so she landed hard on the wooden floor. The list went on and on. So it was with no small amount of trepidation that she met his baby, Darla.

Based on what she knew of him, she would have guessed he would be one of those dads who made everybody else do the work. In fact she had the sneaking suspicion he'd brought her on as some sort of surrogate mother, that he planned to dump the baby on her and resume his party boy lifestyle. She couldn't have been more wrong.

He showed her Darla's routine, all of her likes and dislikes, while being an active, hands-on parent. In fact she only held the baby once that first night, for ten minutes while he took a shower. And it wasn't grudging on his part, like she thought it would be. He approached parenting with all the hands-on enthusiasm of a saint, with full joy and loving attention.

How could she possibly reconcile the two versions of this man? Marlow had no idea, but she was certainly giving it her best effort.

It was possible, she supposed, that he counted the baby as an extension of himself, that he saw caring for her as an extension of caring for him.

In fact, the more she thought about it from this angle, the more sense it made. She thought it was probably also the answer to why he and the mysterious Sterling had been friends for so long. The way Duncan talked about him made it seem as if he viewed Sterling as an extension of himself, too.

So fascinating. And true to his word, he was tidy. The house was spectacular, with amazing bones and a heap of character. True, it was dated and in need of a refresh, but the basic structure was loaded with charm. Darla's room, however, lacked personality completely.

"Girl, we have got to do something about this space," Marlow whispered the first morning of her job. She heard Darla's little coo, and her heart flipped over. *This is it, first day as a real nanny.* Now she stood in the center of the bland white room and peered into the bland white crib, Darla's inquisitive little face staring back at her. "You need color. And texture. Let's see how far we can bend your daddy to your whims to get some of that in here."

Having decided she passed muster, Darla bestowed a beaming and gummy smile on her, instantly lighting her world. And that was the moment Marlow fell in love, with the baby at least. She reached in and picked her up, cradling her close and kissing her cheeks. It was slightly disconcerting how much she looked like Duncan. The resemblance was almost off putting because Marlow certainly had no desire to hold him close or kiss his cheeks. His baby, on the other hand, was innocent of all his mistakes and, as of this moment, completely dependent on her.

She sang her a little song as they descended the stairs, much to Darla's delight. She seemed captivated by Marlow, if the spellbound way she stared at her face was any indication.

"I'm new, huh," Marlow said as she gave Darla her morning bottle. "New is always interesting."

There was no rocking chair, another disappointment. When the bottle was finished, she changed the baby out of her sleep outfit, washed her face and neck, and took her on a tour of the house. Or, to be more specific, Duncan's room. It was the only space she hadn't yet seen, and she was curious.

It didn't yield many surprises. She guessed it would be neat and well organized, and it was. His bed was made, his towel picked up off the floor. Even his shower supplies were at a perfect angle. "Psycho," she whispered. It might have been a hotel room except one small picture on his nightstand, Duncan and a woman, his arm around her neck, she looking more annoyed than in love, as if she were in the act of elbowing him in the gut. Having met Duncan, it didn't come as a surprise. Was she his sister? Despite the woman's annoyance, the photo radiated affection. Duncan didn't seem the type to keep a picture of his sister on his nightstand, but Marlow could assign no other meaning to her, especially because she didn't look like his type. Meaning she wasn't perfect. Her naturally curly hair flew out of her head at all angles. And her face, while pleasant enough, wasn't flawless. Her features were small and delicate, her small nose slightly tipped. She was cute, adorable maybe, but not the supermodel Marlow had imagined. Even Chelsea, his drunken mistake, was much prettier.

"Maybe there's one secret drop of depth in your dad after all," Marlow whispered to Darla, who squealed and kicked in response. "Are you ready to be on the floor, working those muscles?" In response, Darla kicked with more enthusiasm. "I'll take that as a yes."

Withdrawing from Duncan's room, she turned and went downstairs. She set Darla on the floor, spread some toys out, and lay down across from her, smiling when the baby focused all her effort on trying to touch one of the toys. Her frustration when she failed was palpable. Marlow was so intent watching the baby it took her a few minutes to realize someone was in the room, watching her.

With alarm she sat up, hand on her heart. An older man and woman stood staring at her in return, only they were beaming at her.

"Isn't she a doll?" the woman asked.

"She really is, though, if I may ask, who are you people?"

The woman put her hand on the man's arm. "Oh, he didn't tell her, Fred."

"No, he didn't tell her," the man agreed.

"We're Duncan's parents, Fred and Sue." She said the names so quickly together they sounded like one. Fredandsue.

"Oh, I'm so sorry. No, he didn't warn me you'd be stopping by." *Or that you'd let yourselves in. Or that you apparently have a key.* "I'm Marlow."

"We know," the Sue half of Fredandsue answered, her plump body wriggling like an eager puppy. "We're so happy to meet you. We couldn't wait to pop in and say hi." She waved hello, as if they were across a great distance and not two feet apart in a living room. Marlow waved in return, to be friendly.

They stayed for the next three hours, until it was time for Darla's morning nap. It was possible they stayed through that, but Marlow hid upstairs in her room after she put the baby down, almost desperate for some alone time.

When she emerged downstairs an hour later, Darla in hand, they were gone. She gave Darla another bottle, her only food for the time being. Chelsea and Duncan were locked in a battle over when to introduce her to solids. Chelsea wanted to do it the old fashioned way with strained foods, but Duncan was a shockingly strong proponent of baby-led weaning, introducing an older baby to solid foods they could feed themselves. *Duncan will probably win,* Marlow realized. Of the two parents, he definitely had the stronger personality. It wasn't that Chelsea didn't love Darla, anyone could see she did, more that she merely seemed along for the ride, almost glad for Duncan's takeover, this-is-how-we're-doing-it demands.

Duncan arrived home late. Marlow made supper, but she didn't wait for him to eat. He walked in the door and his face lit. "There's my girl." For one wild second Marlow thought he was talking to her, but then she realized she was holding his baby.

He strode forward and reached for Darla who, recognizing him, squealed and kicked in delight. All in all, it was a pleasant greeting to bear witness to and made Marlow smile.

He retrieved his food one handed and sat. Though he was reluctant to let go of Darla, it was obvious eating would soon turn catastrophic, so he ceded control of her back to Marlow who held her close, narrating what Duncan was doing so she would still feel involved.

"Do you think she notices my food?" Duncan asked. "That's one of the signs she's ready for solids."

"Maybe. Earlier today she asked if we had any caviar, so I think she's getting there."

"And she has good taste like her dad," he said, chucking Darla under her double chins. "How did it go today?"

"Good, except she won all my money in poker. I got it back when I took her to the slots, though. Oh, and your parents stopped by." She searched his face to see if this was a surprise, but he seemed to take it in stride.

"They do that now and again."

"Do they have a key?"

"This was the house my mom grew up in. It would be harsh to take away her key," Duncan said.

"A fair point."

"They only stop by every couple of weeks or so. It's not an everyday thing," he said.

She tried not to show her relief. "You don't look like them."

"That's because I'm adopted," he said.

"Really?"

"Yes. They wanted kids desperately, tried forever, finally adopted me."

"So you're the only child of parents who desperately wanted you, who likely spoiled you completely, pampered and adored you, gave in to your every whim, told you every day how special and perfect you are."

"Yes," he said happily.

"The pieces are starting to come together now," she said. At least she'd finally answered the question of his total self-absorption. He'd been in training for it his whole life. "Do you know your biological parents?"

He shook his head.

"Do you want to?"

He shook his head again.

"Why not?"

"It goes back to the overthinking thing. I'm happy with my mom and dad, they're happy with me. Why would I want more?" He finished his food and reached for Darla, snuggling her close and murmuring sweet words of affection.

"Do you think it's possible you've taken such a shine to fatherhood because you secretly have always wanted to belong to someone biologically and now you do?"

He stared hard at Darla, brows lowered in thought. "Yes," he said slowly.

"Hmm," she said, nodding.

He reached over and flicked her knuckle. "You owe me penance for making me be introspective. Go get your guitar and play us a piece."

Without comment, she rose and went upstairs, returning a minute later with her guitar.

CHAPTER 5

The guitar was nice, soft and soothing. It allowed his mind to drift in the best possible way. Duncan was the sort of person who thrived on work pressure, but even so he could feel the tension draining out of him after his long day. He might have fallen asleep, but Marlow spoke.

"I need to ask you something."

"Yes, I will hook up with you, no there cannot be strings," he said.

"Oh, wow. Hold on a second, I need to take a mental shower." She pressed her fingers to her temples a few beats and continued. "I'm going to go on as if those cursed words never came out of your mouth and ask why your daughter's nursery looks like the birthing room in *A Brave New World.*"

He squinted at her, confused by the reference.

"It's sterile. Being that she is much beloved, I would have thought you would have decked it out in some girly fashion."

"Ah. Well, I wanted to, but I've been pretty exhausted. I guess I could go to Ikea in Atlanta next time I'm there, pick some things up." He noted her horrified stare. "What?"

"Ikea?" she drawled.

"Don't tell me you've never heard of it. Was the place you moved from Mars?"

"It doesn't seem to fit in this house," she said.

"Why not?" he asked, sighing. This was going to be one of those girly tirades that made no rational sense, he could tell.

"This house is more than a hundred years old with solid wood trim and pine floors. And you're going to bring composite, pre-fab furniture into it, furniture that is lacking all soul."

"Some people pay priests good money to get the souls out of their furniture," he said and was rewarded when she snorted a laugh.

"You know what I mean."

"No, I actually don't. What are you talking about? I like things nice and new and white. I don't want furniture that's been used by other people. I don't buy used underwear for the same reason."

"That might be the most illogical comparison I have ever heard. You can't compare a hundred year old handcrafted antique to your boxers."

"I think you underestimate how amazing my boxers are," he said, tossing her a wink.

"Oh, yak, I'm living in a frat house of one," she said, pressing her fingers to her temples again. She took a deep breath and tried again. "Why don't you let me decorate Darla's room?"

He scowled. "No way."

"Why not?"

"Because she's my daughter and it's my house and I want to do it."

"But you clearly don't know how, and I'm really good at this sort of thing. Plus she's a girl and I'm a girl, I know about these things. And when are you going to have time or energy?"

"When are you?" he countered.

"I don't have the baby for half the week in the evenings and every other weekend, and this will be fun. Come on, please? I'll be your best nanny." She clasped her hands under her chin and gave him puppy eyes. It didn't work because her eyes were a mix of blue and green. Pretty eyes, he noted, which apparently worked the same on him as brown.

"Fine, but if I hate it, I'm going to redo it in Ikea," he threatened.

"Okay," she agreed, happy now.

"And you have to use low VOC paint because of the fumes."

She gave him a little salute, then appeared to think of something as her head snapped up. "No peeking, though. You have to wait until I'm finished for the big reveal."

He scowled. "I don't like not knowing things."

"Shocking. But if you look, you're going to see it half done and want me to change it because you lack vision. So you have to wait until it's finished."

"Are all nannies this high maintenance?" he asked.

"Only the really good ones," she said.

He flicked his fingers at her. "Play me something to soothe my frazzled nerves." He leaned back, regarding her as she picked out a pleasant little melody. Today her long blond hair was piled up on top of her head in some sort of messy bun situation girls universally favored. Pretty as she was now, she would be extraordinary if she were thinner. "Are you trying to lose weight?"

She shook her head, sighing. "Duncan, you have got to stop saying the quiet part out loud."

"What? I'm not allowed to ask about the…"

She cut him off. "If you say the elephant in the room, I will throw this guitar at your face."

"Fine, I'm not allowed to ask about the most obvious thing?"

"Why does it have to be the most obvious thing?" she asked.

"It just is," he shrugged.

"But that's so unfair. I am so much more than my size, but to guys like you, it's all you ever see."

"So change it. Lose some weight."

"First of all, that's not the point. I am healthy. I work out, I lift weights. I do not have high blood pressure or high cholesterol or diabetes or any of the other things associated with being overweight. So at this point it's about aesthetics, and I am happy with how I look. Why should I starve myself to make you happy?"

"Not me, any guy. Don't you want to date?" he asked.

"Don't you think I do?" she countered.

He tipped his head.

She picked up the tissue box beside her, intending to hurl it at him. But the baby was too nearby and she set it back down again, with a thump that made it crumple. "Not that you've asked, but I have a boyfriend."

"Okay," he said, clearly disbelieving.

She closed her eyes and took a deep breath. "You may have the depth of a drip of water, but not all men do. Some men have the ability to see beyond the extra pounds to the person within. A smoking body isn't everything."

"It's not only about looks. It points to a lack of discipline, a lack of care with personal appearance."

"Why? Because you say so? You already know I work out, we met at the gym. I take plenty of care with my appearance, and I am a very disciplined person. I'm athletic and I eat well, lots of fruits and vegetables."

"Then why are you fat?" he probed.

"I don't know," she said, setting down the guitar to throw up her hands in exasperation. "Why do you have brown hair? It just is. The only time I have ever been thin was when I went on a thousand calorie a day diet, and I was miserable, much too miserable to enjoy life. So I decided long ago I would rather be chubby and enjoy life than skinny and wretched. And then I have people like you heaping it on, trying to make me feel like a failure because I'm not a size six. But let me tell you, you with all your extra height and male metabolism, have absolutely no room to comment on me because you don't know. You *can't* know the struggle of being a woman whose body size is the foremost thought of everyone who meets her, from sun up to sun down, day after day until she dies. So, let me be clear on this, do not ever mention my weight again because, let me assure you, it is absolutely none of your concern."

With that, she clutched her guitar and fled up the stairs.

Duncan remained staring into space. He didn't feel bad, per se. Remorse seemed to be out of his reach on most things. But she had given him a lot to think about. Why did he view her as fat first, a person second? And why did he believe it was a personal failing on her part? She was strong and athletic, he knew that from watching her at the gym and then wrestling with her on the night he hired her. She had already demonstrated, in numerous ways, that she was a hard worker. And yet he persisted in believing she was a lazy ball of flab, even though he knew it was untrue.

He realized, uncomfortably, that he was prejudiced. Growing up in the Deep South, he had been very careful to be sensitive about race. He had a lot of black friends and coworkers, had dated a rainbow's worth of variously tinted women, and tried never to let skin color be a determining factor in anything. To him, it wasn't. He couldn't care less what color people were, nor where they came from, nor what language they spoke. But somewhere along the way he had allowed himself to believe fat shaming was okay, that judging someone by the size of their pants was somehow better and more acceptable than judging them by the color of their skin.

He reached for Darla, snuggling her close in his attempt to override his thoughts. He did not appreciate these little insights into himself, harsh glimpses of his character that made him feel lacking in some way. It was so much easier, so much better to remain blissfully unaware of his flaws.

"You think I'm perfect, don't you?" he whispered to Darla, who cooed happily in response.

Despite his best efforts, he had another little flash of deep thinking. *What if Darla turned out to be fat?* Would he love her any less? No. To him, she would always be perfect, regardless of size, regardless of anything. And maybe that was the point of what Marlow had tried to say. All she wanted was the same consideration, to be seen from the inside out. Hard as it was for him to fathom how that could be possible, from now on he vowed to try.

CHAPTER 6

$\mathcal{H}$e made her cry, drat him and his probing questions.

It wasn't that Marlow believed they would be real friends. Duncan was far too shallow and damaged for that. She liked her friends the same way she liked her pizza—deep dish. But she hadn't expected his cruelty to be aimed at her, hadn't expected to feel the sting of his words as he talked about her weight. He, with his perfect good looks and blinding white teeth, was one more in a long list of people who assured her she would never fit in, if only for the sin of being bigger than they thought she was supposed to be. His words weren't unexpected, but the pain they brought were. For a moment, she had allowed herself to believe there was more to him than met the eye, that somewhere inside was a good man of depth and character. She no longer felt that way.

In response, she ignored him—something easy to do with the long hours he worked—and threw herself into decorating Darla's room. The creative ideas had been flowing since she first spied the space; it was a relief to finally bring them to fruition. She immersed herself in her task, using her time away from the baby to paint, plot, and craft. Duncan skulked outside the room, pouty and perturbed at being kept out of the loop. Approximately once a night he knocked on the door.

"Go away," she commanded and, with a sigh, he did.

"I'm having Sterling and Alby over for dinner on Friday," he told her one morning before he left for work. They had taken to eating breakfast together, but only in the most technical sense. Since it was Darla's normal wakeup time, Marlow saw no need to pussyfoot around until he left, but it wasn't an intimate cozy time. He usually scrolled messages on his phone while she fed Darla her bottle and then stared at her laptop.

"I'll make myself scarce," Marlow promised.

Duncan gave one of his longsuffering sighs, the kind that said she was a supreme idiot due to her lack of ability to read his mind. "They're coming to meet you, dummy."

She leaned to the side and glanced at him around her laptop. "Why?"

"Because you live here and care for my child. They're nosy that way, both of them, all up in my business all the time. I'm the most fascinating piece of their otherwise mundane lives."

"Am I supposed to cook supper?" she asked.

"No, I'm not that kind of employer. We'll buy something and you just need to serve it and clean up," he said and dodged when she threw a wadded napkin at him. "You really lack a sense of humor about your deferential state. We'll get pizza."

"All right," she said, returning to her computer. She could feel Duncan's frown, but she didn't care. Like most vain people, he couldn't stand to be ignored. What he said the first day was true; his boredom threshold was low. He preferred conversation to silence, amusement to inactivity, inane conversation to quiet introspection. He had seemingly noticed that Marlow was ignoring him, and he didn't like it.

Instead of apologizing for his earlier harsh comments, what he said was, "You're not as much fun as you used to be."

"I've matured greatly in the time I've been here," she said. "Time spent with you is aging me like dog years."

He laughed, pleased with her spark of humor, even if it was at his expense. "How long have you and the boyfriend been together?"

She glanced at the clock. Fifteen minutes until he had to leave. Apparently he planned to fill it with chatter. "Four years."

He blinked at her. "And where is he now?"

"Savannah."

"What does he do?"

"Construction by day, music at night."

"He's a performer?" he asked.

"Yes, he is, a very good one."

He studied her in silence a few beats, then, "He's cheating on you."

She closed her laptop. "What? No, he isn't. He's very loyal. You don't even know him."

"No, but I am a man, and I know how we work. Fact, you've been together four years and are not engaged. That means you're never getting married. Fact: you moved here and he didn't. That means he's not vested. Fact: he's in a band and his supposed girlfriend lives a few hours away. He is cheating on you. Better break up with him before he breaks your heart, save some face."

Anger simmered in her throat, choking her. "Do not judge all men by your yardstick. Jensen is not like that, not the kind of guy to go from woman to woman. We have a very sweet, very special relationship, and we are solid."

He put up his hands, either in surrender or as if he was washing himself of her, she couldn't be certain. "I try to be friendly, offer you some brotherly advice, and you get all frowny face."

She pinched the bridge of her nose. "How are you the victim in every scenario? It's uncanny."

"It's a gift," he said, unconcerned. He stood and poured the remainder of the coffee—coffee Marlow had made for herself—into his travel mug and then reached for Darla. She was the one and only bright spot in his favor, the one thing that kept Marlow from stabbing him in his sleep on most days. Seeing him as a dad was a sight to behold. There was no question in anyone's mind that he adored his daughter, almost as much as he adored being a dad. As much as he clearly loved his job, it seemed almost physically painful for him to part from his baby each day, thus he had developed the little goodbye ritual, telling her all the things he hoped she remembered that day, most notably how much she was loved while he cuddled her close and covered her cheeks with kisses. And even though she couldn't understand his words, Darla seemed to take special delight in the routine, if her overly enthusiastic squeals and kicks were any indication.

Finally, he was gone and Marlow breathed a sigh of relief. She and Darla had developed a nice routine by now and it was safe and comfortable. They played for a couple of hours, until it was time for Darla's morning nap, and then Marlow worked on her own project, a secret she kept from everyone.

Her mind kept wandering, though, to Duncan's words. *He's cheating on you.* Of course she couldn't, *shouldn't* pay Duncan any mind. She and Jensen were solid. Weren't they?

She reached for her phone and gave him a call, even though she knew he likely wouldn't pick up. She was doing the insecure girl thing she loathed, calling to check on him, calling to hear his phone ring. She was about to disconnect when his groggy voice answered.

"'Lo."

"Hey, you're not working today?"

"It's pourin' down here," he said. His hand slid over his face, the rasp of his stubble comforting and familiar to her. "What's up?"

"Nothing. I missed you I guess."

"You guess? You're not certain?"

The hint of humor in his tone made her smile in response. "I'm certain."

"How's life at the farm?"

She had sent him some photos of Duncan's house, and he agreed it was spectacular. "It's good, I'm almost done with the baby's room."

He snorted. "You sound like a housewife."

"Is that so bad?" she asked. It had been a while since they discussed marriage. Suddenly she wondered why.

"Yes, when the one you're married to is not me."

"Oh, believe me, you have nothing to worry about from Duncan."

"Hideous, is he?"

She purposely hadn't sent him a picture of Duncan, not wanting him to know exactly how devastatingly handsome her new boss/roommate was. Not that it mattered, since he was so unattractive on the inside. "He's...something." The conversation lulled to silence that felt strangely awkward or expectant. Or maybe Marlow was sensitive to any disturbance now, thanks to Duncan's harsh words. "It's hard to be apart."

"I know, but it's temporary, right? You're coming back eventually, after you decide your next step."

"Right, yes." She had left with the excuse that she needed to figure some things out, career wise, take a step back and get herself together. That was still true, although taking a job as a nanny felt like a step back. Or if not back, at least in the wrong direction.

"Marlow, baby, you sound sad. What is this about? Do I need to come up there and kiss you good?"

"Yes, please."

"How about Friday?"

"Ugh, I'm committed to a dinner with my boss and his friends. Saturday?"

"I have a gig. Sunday?"

"Yes. Sunday is perfect. How long can you stay?"

"Just the day, unfortunately. I'm starting a new construction project on Monday, bright and early, barring rain, of course." Something buzzed or chirped in the background. "I've gotta go, but I will see you on Sunday."

"I can hardly wait," Marlow said, heart thudding. "I love you."

"You too."

They disconnected and she sat staring at her phone with a smile. Would a guy who was cheating drive three hours to visit for an afternoon? No. *Take that, Duncan, and keep your ill-founded opinions to yourself.*

CHAPTER 7

$\mathcal{D}$uncan was oddly nervous about the dinner with Sterling and Alby. Why, though? It was only Marlow. Perhaps because Sterling's approval meant so much to him he wouldn't be able to keep her as a nanny if things didn't go well. And even though it was hypothetical, the thought hurt somehow. He didn't want to let go of Marlow. He had gotten used to her, liked having another grownup in the house. Plus she was amazing with Darla, exactly as he had imagined, the nanny of his dreams. She acted like a mom to her in all the ways, tender, loving, patient, attentive. Darla was always clean, dressed, content. He wasn't with them during the day, but he would know if his baby was unhappy, would see the signs of stress or upset in her little face.

Secretly, or perhaps not so secretly, he wondered if she was an even better mom to Darla than Chelsea was. Not that he spent enough time with Chelsea to know. They saw each other twice a week to exchange the baby, during which time their conversation was limited to pertinent information relating to Darla. *Her gums are puffy,* was the most he'd heard her say in the last month. And he was perfectly fine with that.

He picked up the pizzas on his way home. When he walked in, the house smelled like chocolate. "What smells so amazing?" he asked. He glanced toward Darla's empty bouncy seat with a pang. He hated the weekends she was with Chelsea, longed desperately to hear her squeals of delight at his arrival. *All women should react that way to me,* he noted absently. *Who am I kidding? They do.*

"I made brownies and homemade ice cream," Marlow said, wiping down the already immaculate kitchen counters. It was obvious she had cleaned. They were both tidy, but she had clearly gone over and above in her efforts to make everything look nice, and he felt touched by her thoughtfulness.

"Aw, that was sweet. You didn't have to."

"It's Georgia, Duncan. If you don't serve sugar with supper, you get booted from the state."

"That's probably so," he agreed. Marlow finally faced him and he resisted the urge to do a double take. In addition to putting in extra effort with the house, she had put in extra effort with her appearance. She looked so good on a normal basis, he didn't realize it was her minimum. Now she was wearing full makeup, her hair down and curly. "You look nice." Understatement, she looked gorgeous.

"Thank you," she said, giving her hair a self-conscious pat.

A knock sounded on the door and Duncan turned to answer. He and Sterling weren't in the habit of knocking before they entered. The formality was for Marlow's sake. He found it both endearing and unnerving. He appreciated it, but he also wished they wouldn't. It was only Marlow, nothing significant in that. Things hadn't changed, wouldn't change. Especially not between him and Sterling; Duncan couldn't take it.

"Hey, y'all, come in," Duncan said.

"Are we early?" Alby asked worriedly. She was that type of person who was always worried about being in the way or making another person uncomfortable. Duncan couldn't imagine. If it had been anyone but Alby, he probably would have found it annoying, but they had known each other since they were five, and she was good people.

"No, sweetheart, you're perfectly on time," he said, reaching out to give her a hug. He was so relieved with Sterling's choice of mate that it made him uncharacteristically effusive. Sterling had dated some stunners over the years, Chelsea included. Duncan had long secretly feared that he would harbor a thing for whomever Sterling ended up with, that he would always pine for what his best friend had. There was no pining for Alby, however. Not that she wasn't attractive. She was cute and, to his shock, had a nice body, too. But she was so *Alby* he could never see her as anything but the girl he'd known forever. She was probably as close as he would ever get to having a sister, and that was the extent of his feelings for her, sisterly affection. Almost but not quite protective. In Sterling's stead, Duncan would be most upset if anyone ever hurt his little friend.

Marlow must have entered the room because attention shifted toward the kitchen. Duncan eyed Sterling who did an almost comedic double take before shooting Duncan a look. Despite his continued silence, Duncan had no trouble interpreting. *Why didn't you tell me she was hot?*

Duncan turned to survey Marlow. Was she hot? She had the face and hair, for certain. Of course Sterling wouldn't mind the body, both because he had Alby and he'd always been good that way.

"Oh," Alby said, taking a step forward and stopping short, hands tucked under her chin.

"She wants to hug you," Duncan translated.

"Well sure," Marlow said and, beaming, pulled the smaller Alby into a swallowing hug.

"You're not a hugger," Duncan said, affronted.

"Of course I am," Marlow said.

"You don't hug me," he argued.

"That's how you get possessed, by touching unholy relics," she said, and Sterling laughed hard.

"You must be hangry. That's the only way I can account for speaking to your employer thus," Duncan said.

"Then you must be hangry all the other minutes of the day," she countered.

"We're going to have to find a way to keep you on after Darla outgrows a nanny," Sterling said, stepping forward to give her hand an earnest shake. "Get on it, Albertine."

"Alby's loaded," Duncan explained in a whispered aside.

"So are you," Marlow whispered in return.

"No, I'm middle-of-nowhere Georgia rich. She's summer on the Riviera with Clooney wealthy," he explained.

"Well, thank you, Duncan. That's exactly the first thing I want people to know about me," Alby said, linking her arm with his. "And to be fair, I've only lunched with Clooney three or four times."

"Sterling started it," he said.

"I'll deal with him later," Alby said, tossing her fiancé a smile.

"Alby, gross. I don't need those images in my head," Duncan said, pressing his hands to his ears.

"Remember junior year when I drove you and Anna Mosby home from my house after homecoming? Believe me when I tell you I owed you," Alby said, giving his arm a squeeze.

He squinted. "I don't remember, actually."

"It'll probably come out in therapy someday. For both of us," she said.

He laughed and deposited her in the kitchen. Marlow had already set out plates and drinks. They filled their plates and sat to eat.

"Marlow, where do you come from?" Sterling asked.

"Down toward Savannah," Marlow said.

"What brought you up this way?" Alby asked.

"My dad got a job up here."

"And what does he do?" Sterling asked.

"He's a pastor."

"You never told me that," Duncan said.

"You never asked," she returned.

"Do I have to draw every piece of information out of you like a tooth extraction?" he groused.

She placed a brownie on his plate. Placated, he returned to eating.

"Was childcare what you always wanted to do?" Alby asked.

"In a manner of speaking. I was an education major in college, but older grades. I taught high school for three years in Savannah."

"What?" Duncan expelled, annoyed all over again.

"Why did you quit, if you don't mind my asking," Sterling said.

"It was different than I thought it would be. When my parents moved, it seemed like a good time to take a step back, reassess. I was planning to get my substitute certificate when Duncan tackled me."

"I wish you were speaking hypothetically, but knowing Duncan I'm going to guess not," Sterling said. He reached for the uneaten third of Alby's pizza and polished it off.

"She did not go down easy," Duncan said with satisfaction, reaching for Marlow's uneaten pizza.

She smacked his fingers. "If you want to keep that hand, you better never come between me and my food again."

"She has a boyfriend," Duncan tossed out, shaking out his injured fingers. "In Savannah. So, you know, they're definitely going to last." He gave an "oof" of pain and crumpled when she jabbed him in the ribs.

"How long have you been together?" Alby asked, her gentle tone working to tamp down some of the annoyance now circulating in the room.

"Four years."

"How did you meet?" Sterling asked.

"He was working on the crew of an event I was involved in," she said.

Alerted by her vague tone, Duncan's eyes narrowed. "What event?"

"Beauty pageant," she murmured, not lifting her eyes from her pizza.

"Which pageant?" he asked. The skepticism in his tone made her look up and shoot daggers at him.

"Miss Georgia."

"I don't keep up on that sort of thing. Did you win?" Alby asked.

Marlow broke off scowling at Duncan to smile at her. "No, but I was the runner up."

"You're just full of secrets tonight, aren't you?" Duncan asked.

"No, I'm full of public information for anyone not self-involved enough to seek it," she said, reaching to his plate to polish off his uneaten portion of pizza. Across the table, Sterling snickered.

"I maybe don't like you without Darla," Duncan muttered.

"And what about you two?" Marlow said, ignoring Duncan and turning her attention to Sterling and Alby. "Were you high school sweethearts?"

"I wish," Sterling said, reaching over to give Alby's leg a squeeze. "We didn't reconnect until recently."

"Duncan said you own the bookstore in town. Sadly, I haven't been yet, but it's on my list of places to visit," Marlow said.

"It's amazing," Alby gushed. "I mean, seriously. Sterling has done so much work. It's becoming quite the destination."

"It's my second love," Sterling said, then sat up as if thinking of something. "Hey, you should bring Darla for story time."

Marlow gasped. "I would love that. I definitely will."

"You do story time?" Duncan asked.

"No, but Miss Inez does."

"Miss Inez," Duncan said, all enthusiasm. "Maybe *I'll* come to story time."

"You should both go," Alby declared. "Duncan, you haven't been since Sterling renovated."

"It's a bookstore, Alby. Not my natural habitat."

"How are you two friends?" Marlow asked.

"Because Sterling is that rare breed who successfully straddled the jock/nerd gap," Alby said, patting his knee now.

"Hey, me too," Marlow said. She held her fist out for a bump, and Sterling tapped it.

"It's not like I was a moron," Duncan said, holding up his hand like a stop sign to Marlow before she could chime in with a comment.

"You're very smart," Alby soothed. "But you've never been a dedicated reader, never went beyond what you had to do for school."

"Alby, you're such a good mom," Duncan said, giving her a brief, yet tight squeeze.

"Don't break her," Sterling warned.

"You worry too much," Duncan said, rolling his eyes. "Alby's tough stuff. Like Marlow." He gave her bicep a little shove.

"You have to be tough to play lacrosse," she said, earning an annoyed eye roll from Duncan.

The remainder of the night was light and casual, only feeling slightly odd when they walked Sterling and Alby to the door as if they were a couple. "They're sweet," Marlow said, smiling fondly.

"Hmm," Duncan replied. He pivoted into the kitchen and began cleaning up. Marlow followed.

"Stop giving me the silent treatment," she said.

"What? Is it bothersome when your roommate ignores you? I can't imagine."

"I had reason; you don't," she said.

He whirled on her. "Are you joking? You've been living here for weeks and it's like I don't even know you. Like the fact that you have a degree and were a teacher."

"It was on the resume I gave you," she said, indignant.

He waved her away. "No one reads resumes."

"This is so you, Duncan. I have been right here this whole time, and you've asked me nothing. You had a physical copy of my education and work history on file, and yet you blame me because you didn't read it. You make me crazy, you really, really do."

Far from being peeved, he was now smiling. "Then I guess we're even." She was still seething, he could tell. He surprised them both by stepping forward and hugging her. "As penance for withholding information, you have to hug me because I'm a hugger, too, and when Darla is at Chelsea's I go through affection withdrawal."

For a few beats, she held herself stiffly away, and then she gave in and hugged him. "Do not think this means I like you," she said, voice muffled against his shoulder.

"You have to. My circle is small, but it's tight. And I hate, *hate* not knowing what's going on with my friends. So if there's anything else you'd like to add, now is the time."

"Jensen is coming on Sunday."

It took him a minute to remember who Jensen was. The boyfriend, of course. "Good, I want to meet him, give him my stamp of approval."

She laughed. "You goof, it's the other way around."

He pulled back slightly so he could see her face. "I ask you, Marlow. Who wouldn't approve of me?"

"Ugh," she replied, giving him a shove and walking away.

He must be more affection deprived than he realized, because he had to fight the temptation to pull her back.

CHAPTER 8

On Saturday Marlow woke with purpose.

"It's finished," she said at breakfast.

Duncan glanced up from his phone, a blank expression on his handsome face. "You and the boyfriend? Told you so."

She pinched the bridge of her nose. She was going to get a permanent imprint. "The nursery."

He set down his phone. "Let's go."

"Let me lead," she called, hurrying behind him.

"Never," he called, picking up the pace.

She picked up her pace, too, until it became an all out sprint to the baby's room. They reached for the handle together and literally fell inside, landing in an untidy heap.

Duncan was the first to recover, sitting up on his hands and knees, mouth agape. She tried to see it anew through his eyes, shades of violet and moss, an enchanted forest. She'd painted a mural on one wall, with a magical tree stuffed with fairies, toadstools, and gnomes.

"You did it," he said at last.

"Did what?"

"Made it perfect." He sat back, falling hard onto his bottom. "She's going to love it."

"Eventually, I hope. She's a bit young yet."

He shook his head vaguely, still looking a bit stunned. "Not Darla."

"Who?" she asked, but he didn't answer.

"Where did this furniture come from?"

She'd added an antique oak dresser, a rocking chair, and a painted miniature wardrobe for play clothes. "Thrift store."

"And the accessories?" He eyed the chunky blanket and macramé wall hanging.

"I made them."

"It's so great," he breathed, sounding awed.

"Better than Ikea?" she couldn't help but ask.

He snagged her around the neck and pulled her alongside him. "Don't be smug."

They surveyed the room in silence a few minutes. "Hey, know what I want?" he eventually asked.

"Everything, on a silver platter?" she guessed.

"Yes, but specific to this moment. I want to see the beauty pageant picture."

Her nose wrinkled. "I don't even know if I still have it."

"Of course you do. Girls always keep pictures where they look good."

She gave him a shove, mostly for being right.

"Come on, get it or I'll keep bugging you. You know I'll wear you down eventually."

It was true, he was the consummate salesman. If his sparkling personality didn't make the sale, his undying persistence did. With a longsuffering sigh she went to her room, rooted in her memory box, and retrieved the picture. She handed it to Duncan, who remained in the nursery, and sat cross-legged on the floor beside him.

He stared at the picture, whistling appreciatively. "Who on earth could you possibly have lost to?"

She pointed to the girl beside her.

"Oh, right. She is prettier." Grinning, he dodged her blow and continued. "But only slightly. Seriously, I would have voted for you."

"I wouldn't have," she said.

"Why not?" he asked.

"I didn't much like me then."

"Why not?"

"Because look at me, look at my eyes. I was so…"

"Sad? Insecure?" he guessed, squinting hard at the picture.

"Hungry."

He laughed.

"I'm serious. I was starving all the time, trying so hard to fit the image. I'm five ten, worked out twice a day, and tried to exist on a thousand calories of steamed chicken and vegetables. It was so hard, so not worth it. I…" she paused and took a breath. "I came so close to losing myself."

"How so?"

"Because I was becoming obsessive with the working out, the starvation. The perfectionism began to take control. There were some days when I only drank a glass of juice, when I worked out for hours on end. I could feel myself spiraling away. I stopped having fun, stopped *being* fun. Everything became about the goal, fitting into the dress, looking the part. There was so much pressure."

"What happened to bring about the change?" he asked.

"One of the pageant doctors offered me a prescription for Adderall. He said I wouldn't have to work so hard on my weight, would have more energy, less appetite. It sounded like a dream, so of course I took it." Duncan winced. Being in pharmaceuticals, he understood the risks. "It was glorious, exactly as he said. For the first time in my life, I wasn't hungry. I had so much energy. Of course I also stopped sleeping and my anxiety went through the roof, but who cared? I was skinny. But being the perfectionist I am, a little wasn't good enough. I began crushing and snorting it, a trick I learned from a ballerina I knew."

"Oh, geez," Duncan said, wincing harder.

"Right. I had just started seeing Jensen then. He caught me and was rightfully appalled. He wanted me to get help. I told him he was nuts. He said unless or until I sought help, he wouldn't have anything to do with me, and he meant it. Harsh, but it was the wakeup I needed. I stopped taking the drug, started going to counseling, got my life back on track. Of course I started gaining weight the minute I stopped dieting obsessively, and that was very hard. But by then I had also gained enough perspective to understand it was better to be chubby and alive than skinny and dead."

"Can't there be a happy medium?" Duncan asked.

She gave him a rueful smile, reading his mind. He wanted her to be skinny, she knew, even if he didn't want her to be sad and obsessive. "If so, I haven't found it."

He set the picture aside with an uncharacteristically somber expression. "Well, then, I suppose I'd rather have you like this."

She laughed. "Thank you so much for your permission."

He pressed a palm to his chest. "I'm your employer. You need my permission for everything."

She clasped her hands in a pleading expression. "Kind sir, would you permit me to go to your friend's bookstore today?"

He grimaced. "A bookstore? On a Saturday? Nerd."

Rolling her eyes, she stood and attempted to walk away, but he followed. "I want to come too," he declared.

"Nerd," she said.

"Apparently it's contagious."

"For that to be true, I would have to have seen you read something in the last few weeks," she said.

"I read plenty," he argued.

"Putting the closed caption on when you watch ESPN does not count," she said.

"Who made you the literature police?" he demanded, smiling when she laughed. "If I go to the bookstore with you, you have to go to the gym with me."

"I'm not the one demanding to tag along to the bookstore," she reminded him.

"You are so petty," he said. "Pack for the gym, I'm not stopping back here."

"It's your world, Duncan, and we're all along for the ride," she said.

"Now you're getting it." He swatted her on the backside, wincing when she reared back and kicked him hard in the shin.

"You are a lawsuit waiting to happen," she said.

"You think I'm this charming with everyone? Nah, it's all you, girl."

"Aren't I the lucky one?"

He hooked an arm around her neck and squeezed. "It's about time you realized."

CHAPTER 9

"Odd," Duncan remarked as he drove past Sterling's bookstore.

"The shape of your head? I thought so at first, but after a while you start not to notice," Marlow replied.

"There's no parking," he noted, ignoring her. He pretended to be annoyed by her teasing, but really he liked it. In all his life, Birdie was the only other woman who had ever teased him. To Duncan, it was a sign not only of belonging, but a signal they could hold their own. He wasn't unaware of the strength of his personality. Most women were too easy to steamroll.

"Must be a popular place," she said, all enthusiasm, hand on the door, ready to spring.

"The bookstore?" he intoned, but too late, she was already dodging ahead, leaving him to once again jog to catch up.

"Can't you let me lead, just once?"

"Never," she replied, shoving him aside to open the door to the shop. Then they both tumbled inside and stopped short. "Oh, my goodness."

"What on earth?" Duncan asked in the same awed tone. Last time he was at Sterling's store, it had been a cavernous white space, bare except for the shelves lining each wall, stacked with books. Empty in all the ways, void of customers. Now it was apparently Grand Central of middle Georgia. There were people everywhere, all ages. A group of old ladies sat knitting in the far corner. Up front, children zoomed and laughed. On the opposite side of the room, a man held court in front of at least thirty people who paused occasionally to laugh at something he said. And the space itself had been transformed to a quiet riot of colors, deep hues that called to mind old libraries in England, except the kids' section that was a bright blend of primary colors.

"It's an author signing," Marlow whispered excitedly, tugging his sleeve as she looked at the man and his entourage.

"Which author?" Duncan asked, not that he would know the difference. The last book he read was for college, and even then he'd tried to get Birdie to do it for him.

"Does it matter?" Still tugging his sleeve, she led him to the far side of the room. The man droned on about something or other. Duncan let his eyes wander, feeling no small amount of annoyance with Sterling. Why hadn't he mentioned he was renovating the shop? Why hadn't he said how well it was doing now?

The man finished his talk. Beside him Marlow applauded and then elbowed him. "Stop scowling. You're going to frighten the children and old ladies."

"I didn't know it was like this," Duncan said, motioning to the bustling space. "I didn't know he did such an extensive overhaul and renovation. He never told me."

Marlow quirked an eyebrow at him. Now that he knew she had been a teacher, he had a name for the expression. "Didn't he?"

He started to say no and then remembered that Sterling had met with a bookshop owner from Atlanta, some bigwig friend of Alby's who decided to mentor him. And he *might* have mentioned once or twice that he was extra busy. And, okay, there was a month there where the store was closed for renovation. And it was possible Sterling invited him to the grand re-opening and he forgot.

Marlow leaned close to whisper. "You are never more attractive than when you realize you're wrong."

He leaned close to whisper in return. "That's a blatant lie. I'm never not attractive."

She snorted and linked her arm with his, tugging him forward to explore the rest of the shop. Duncan saw it with fresh eyes, understood all the work and love his friend had put into it so that by the time the store cleared enough for them to catch sight of Sterling, he was feeling overwhelmed to the point of mutism.

"You got Duncan to go to a bookstore. Might have to call you the miracle worker," Sterling said, easing close to speak to Marlow who beamed at him.

"Hey, Sterling. Congratulations on this place. It's incredible, I love it so much. It's exactly what a bookstore should be."

"Thank you. It's been a lot of work, but I had a lot of help, most notably from Alby."

Duncan looked away. He should have been there to help, to do whatever necessary to make Sterling's dream come true. Why hadn't he? True, he had been busy and overwhelmed with the baby, but he had every other weekend free.

"What's wrong with you?" Sterling asked, eyeing him.

"Nothing, I...I'm really proud of you. This is amazing. It's good to see you living your dream. I'm sorry I wasn't more a part of it."

"Thanks," Sterling said, rubbing the back of his neck, his tell that he was uncomfortable. "You've had a lot going on yourself, with Darla."

He was letting him off too easy, Duncan knew. He could at least have been a better listener, had he not been so immersed in his own life and exhaustion. Well, no more. From now on, he was going to be a proponent of Sterling's store, his number one fan. "Do you have cards? I can give them to my clients. I have a lot of readers on my route."

Sterling blinked at him. "Yeah, that would be great, thanks. Hold on, I'll get them." He disappeared. Marlow linked her arm with his and pressed her hand to his heart.

"You might turn out to be a real boy yet, Pinocchio."

"Let's get you to the gym so you can prove you're not a real girl," he said.

"And we're back," she said, dropping his arm and returning her attention to the book selection in front of her.

She bought two horror books and they went to the gym. "You going to do the weights with me?" Duncan asked.

"That was the plan," she said, reaching in her bag for her gloves.

"I don't think you're pressing enough. Let's add twenty pounds."

"Bring it," she said, flexing her hands.

It was hard not to contrast her with Birdie then. Birdie was terrified of the gym, not the least bit athletic. He'd always held a certain worry in the back of his mind that he might break her. In fact he almost had when he attempted to make her lift weights. It had been galling to have Hayden Paxton step in and rescue her. But Marlow did not need a rescue. Able and willing to push herself, she was always ready for the next physical challenge, an athlete's athlete. Duncan liked that about her, liked a lot of things about her, if he were being honest. It was almost like being with Sterling, and that was probably the highest compliment he could ever pay anyone.

She did her reps and spotted him while he did his and then they decided it would be more fun to run outside instead of do their cardio at the gym. They drove the car home and ran a few miles, silently challenging each other to go farther, faster, to push harder without complaining.

They showered and met back up on the couch for leftover pizza and a movie.

"Why are you holding my remote?" Duncan demanded, hand extended.

She clutched it closer. "It's my turn to choose."

"It's my house and my TV."

"Don't be bombastic. Besides, I rented a movie and I need to get my money's worth."

He plopped down beside her, too tired and hungry to argue. "What movie?"

"You're going to love it," she said, tone cryptic.

He did not love it. Marlow was a horror fan; Duncan was not. "How can you stand this stuff?" he asked, hand over his eyes as yet another character was dismembered by a chainsaw.

"If you embrace your fears, they can't get you. Man up, Shepherd," she encouraged, patting his leg.

"Does your boyfriend like this stuff?" he asked.

"Nope. But he encourages me to like it because he realizes I'm my own person, and that's okay."

Duncan thought it more likely he didn't care enough to notice what she watched, nor with whom. He opened his mouth to say as much and thought better of it. Marlow had enough going on without him antagonizing her over her lackluster boyfriend.

He pressed his lips together and felt an odd sensation: self-satisfaction. No doubt about it, he was definitely growing as a person. Birdie would be proud.

The next morning he forgot the boyfriend was coming until Marlow emerged from her room dressed to the nines with full hair and makeup.

"How come you only get dolled up for other people?" he asked, tone resentful.

"Why would I get dressed up for you?" she countered.

"Good manners," he said and was rewarded when she laughed.

"If all you ever see is the body, it doesn't really matter what the face and hair are doing, does it?" she countered.

"I don't like that," he said, waving his drippy milk spoon at her.

"Being confronted with your own flaws? I can't imagine you would."

"I suppose the boyfriend is fine with the weight," he mused.

"Since the weight has been here for three years of our relationship, I suppose so," she said.

He heard the tiniest note of insecurity in her tone but decided not to call her on it. No doubt about it, he was definitely mature now.

"I know you ate the last of the brownies after I went to bed last night," Marlow accused, pointing her spoon at him.

He stuck out his tongue at her. *Mostly mature,* he thought. Perhaps there was a bit of wiggle room.

The boyfriend arrived soon after. Duncan hovered in the doorway of the living room, blatantly observing their greeting. He was almost morbidly curious about the man. What kind of person would Marlow be with?

"My girl," Jensen greeted her, wrapping her in a swallowing hug she heartily returned. He was tall, taller than Duncan, without being overly stretched out. His shoulders were broad and well muscled, the kind of physique that comes from physical labor. His hair was sandy and too long, eyes brown, beard stubbled face. He wore a vintage Nirvana t-shirt and looked like the kind of guy who would argue to the death that vinyl records were the only real way to partake of music. Right away Duncan realized that, while they were definitely opposites, the guy was not a loser. He was that type of guy beloved by a certain kind of girl, the kind of girl who usually looked down on jocks like Duncan. Artsy girls, smart girls. They always went for the singers, artists, and musicians.

"I'm so glad to see you," Marlow gushed, standing on her toes to kiss him. The greeting might have gone on, but they both seemed to realize Duncan was lurking in the doorway, ogling them. "Jensen, this is Duncan." She took Jensen's hand and led him proudly forward, as if she had personally created him and needed to show him off.

"How do you do," Duncan said, striding forward, hand outstretched.

"Sir," Jensen replied, tone friendly but formal.

"Call me Duncan. We're pretty casual around here," he said, tossing Marlow a wink. It had been an unconscious gesture on his part, but Marlow rolled her eyes as if he'd meant it as a power play. Jensen seemed either not to notice or not to care as his eyes scanned the interior of the farmhouse.

"This is some place you have here."

"Thank you," Duncan said. "Make sure Marlow shows you the baby's room. She did a bang up job on it."

"Yes, come look," Marlow pled, tugging him away. They disappeared upstairs and Duncan turned in a circle, wondering what to do with himself for the remainder of the day. Sterling had a thing with Alby, Darla was with Chelsea for a few more hours, and Marlow would be occupied with Jensen. Duncan was out of people, and he didn't like it.

After a while, Jensen and Marlow went out. They didn't say where, and he didn't ask. He puttered, napped, basically wallowed in his aloneness until, hours later, Jensen and Marlow returned.

"Is there still ice cream left or did you hog all that, too?" Marlow greeted him.

"I haven't eaten it yet, but I've got dibs," Duncan said. In truth, he'd forgotten about the ice cream. But he knew she loved it and took pleasure in annoying her.

"Fight me," she said, disappearing into the kitchen, Jensen trailing her.

They returned a few minutes later, bowls in hand. Marlow put a bowl in his hands, too, and they all sat down like civilized people.

"Marlow tells me you're a musician," Duncan said around bites of his ice cream.

"Yes, sir," Jensen agreed.

Duncan couldn't get a read on him. Was he calling him sir in deference to his slightly advanced age? To his position as Marlow's employer? Or, third option, to annoy him?

"What kind of stuff do you play?"

"Indie stuff, for my own pleasure. But most people don't have good enough taste to enjoy it. So I end up doing a lot of covers for gigs," Jensen said.

"Marlow's musical too," Duncan noted.

"Yes, sir."

"Do you two ever play together?" he asked.

Jensen and Marlow looked at each other, smiling. "Whenever possible," Marlow replied.

"Play something for me now," Duncan said.

"I'm going to get you a dancing chicken. That way you can be entertained whenever you want," Marlow said, but she reached for her guitar nonetheless. And then handed it to Jensen as she sat at the piano.

"I didn't know you played the piano, too," Duncan said, annoyed to once again be left out of the loop.

"My dad's a pastor. It's the law," she said.

He wondered what that meant but didn't ask because Jensen was tuning up and he was genuinely curious to hear them. They started playing and singing some soft love song, watching each other as they sang harmony. The sight and sound of them caused an odd, unfamiliar ache in Duncan. This was what he'd dreamed of with Birdie, the same sort of togetherness that spoke of familiarity and belonging. Maybe they would have found it if she'd stayed; maybe they'd get the chance to find it again.

"That was very nice," he said softly when they were finished, feeling like an interloper. It was time for Jensen to leave after that. He and Duncan said a polite goodbye and Marlow walked him outside. When she returned, he could tell she was secretly curious to hear his opinion of Jensen.

"Seems like a nice guy," he commented. She sagged slightly, as if in relief. "Talented," he added.

"Yes, he is. Very."

Duncan nodded his agreement. "There's something majorly wrong with him, though."

She froze and faced him, scowling. "What?"

"He's not jealous of me at all. That's not normal."

She laughed, relieved. "Duncan, you're so bizarre. Why would he be jealous of you?"

"Uh, hello, have you seen me? Also, we live together, we're friends. We spend a lot of time together."

"He's not jealous of you because there is nothing to be jealous of, because we have zero chemistry."

He leaned forward and kissed her. She gave him a hard shove away. "What was that?" she exclaimed.

"You said we had zero chemistry. I was testing it. I'd say we're at about a one, maybe a two."

She pressed her hands to her temples.

"What are you doing?" he asked.

"Trying to tamp down my rage so I don't murder you," she said.

"That kind of passionate anger notches it up to a three," he said.

She growled and stormed up the stairs. Chelsea arrived then and handed a squealing Darla over. Cuddling her, Duncan carried her to the couch and sat down. "I'll tell you a secret, baby," he whispered, eyes darting to the stairs to make certain Marlow was still out of sight. "It was a solid seven."

CHAPTER 10

"Can I use your laptop?"

Marlow startled like a criminal, closing her computer with a snap. "Why?"

"I'm running a few high profile Nigerian scams, and I don't want to leave a trail. Or I'd like to make a call and I left mine at work."

"Why not use your phone?" she asked.

"It's the type of call that needs the full screen experience. What is the big deal? Do you want to put a meter on it, charge me a dime a minute?" He reached in his pocket, as if for change, even though he hated change and never carried it. Clinking change reminded him of his dad, an old man sound.

"All right, hold on a second." She opened the laptop and clicked a few things, closing boxes so only her desktop screen remained.

"What are you guarding over there? State secrets?"

"It's my secret plot to throw you over and take charge of this house. Step one, make you dependent on my laptop, check." She handed him the computer and reached for the baby. "Want me to take her so you can be free to talk?"

He clutched the baby closer. "No, thanks. It's the kind of call that requires a baby."

"Curiouser and curiouser," she said, then leaning in to speak to Darla, "Don't let him sell you. I have dibs."

"Ha, trafficking jokes pertaining to my daughter are hilarious. Away with you," he said, kicking the air behind her as she disappeared upstairs. He waited until she was officially gone before sitting and opening a window.

Birdie appeared right away. Her hair took up two thirds the frame and he smiled, wishing he were there in person to push it away, knowing it would only spring back again. "Hey, girl."

"Hey," she said, waving both hands. She leaned in slightly, focusing on Darla, as he knew she would. "Oh, my goodness, Duncan. She gets more beautiful every time I see her."

"I know, right?"

"You can't know how much I want to see her in person and kiss those cheeks." She leaned forward again, sniffing. "I can almost smell her. I love her."

"She loves you, too." *So do I. Come back. Marry me.* He cleared his throat. "What's new on the other side of the world? You look good." *You look amazing. I adore you.* "All tan and whatnot."

She waved her hand. Birdie was expressive that way, always using every part of her body and face to make a point. "That's generous. You know I'm too pale to actually tan. I think I've added another layer of freckles though." She scrubbed her nose.

"Cute." He cleared his throat again. "Anyway, what's new? How's the job?"

"It's good. I think I'm finally getting the hang of it, now that my first year is almost over." She rolled her eyes, smiling.

"Nah, I bet you were great from the get go. Are you ready to come home?"

"Yes, I miss everyone so much, plus peanut butter and chocolate chip cookies, although the food here is amazing, seriously. I'm going to have to cook for y'all. Hayden says it's going to take a month for all the garlic to leave our pores. He's definitely looking forward to a cheeseburger."

"Hmm," Duncan said, nodding, trying to mask the fact that any mention of her boyfriend made his heart freeze.

"How are you getting on? Sterling said he met your new nanny. Side note, I can't believe you have a nanny. So grown up and fancy."

"I've changed," he said, wishing it were true. "What'd he say about her?" How had Sterling described Marlow to Birdie?

"That she's a lot of fun and he liked her a lot, that she keeps you on your toes."

"It's true, she does," Duncan agreed then, wondering if Sterling had also related Marlow's good looks, hastened to add, "I met her boyfriend last weekend."

"Did you like him?"

"Yeah, he seemed okay, except he's a musician." He pretended to gag and she laughed.

"Sounds like you two will be BFFs soon," Birdie mused.

"You know me, I'm a Renaissance Man," he said.

"Yeah, I know you," she said, smiling. The tone of her voice was more affectionate than lovestruck, to his disappointment. He started to say something else, but her attention was called off camera.

"Oh, no, I'm so sorry, Duncan, but I have to cut this short, a work thing. I'm pretty much always on the job. Thank you for calling, I'm so excited to be home and give everyone a big hug and finally see that sweet baby of yours in person."

"Me, too, and I…"

Too late, she was gone.

"Love you completely, might die if things don't work out between us," he whispered to the blank screen.

When Marlow arrived a few minutes later, he was still staring blankly, absently bouncing Darla who seemed undaunted in her unsuccessful attempts to grab the computer.

"Is your call done?" Marlow whispered.

"Yes."

She sat down beside him, staring at his face. "What's wrong with you?"

"Nothing."

"Oh, okay. Liar."

He let out a breath and shook his head slowly. The baby was now lunging for her. She took her, kissing her cheeks while Darla squealed.

"Duncan, I'm pretty good at the advice thing," she said.

"I don't know where to begin," he said.

"At the beginning," she urged, and so he did. He started with his childhood, how he, Sterling, and Birdie had been so close, like family, how his feelings for Birdie had turned from annoyance to adoration so subtly he didn't know when or how it happened, how he had loved her silently from afar for as long as he could remember, how they'd come so close to making it work, only to have it ripped away.

"So you were together and she ran away, just like that?"

It was possible he had edited the story slightly to make himself more heroic. "Well, we had a bit of a falling out. It was hard for her, with Darla. Chelsea was Sterling's girlfriend, after all. And even though she and I had our thing before Birdie and I got together, she felt caught in the middle. You know, she's loyal like that."

She was frowning, and he feared he'd given her a bad impression of Birdie, but, no, she was merely thinking. "Then go get her. She probably left because she needed some space, but now that she's had time to think and cool down, she's probably ready to rekindle."

"She has a boyfriend," he said miserably.

"So," Marlow surprised him by her cavalier attitude. "What is some random guy she met in the Mediterranean to a hometown guy she grew up with? You have longevity and locality on your side. That guy, he's a flash in the pan."

He should definitely tell her about Hayden, should explain that he was, in fact, local, that he and Birdie had been friends, that Hayden had been the one to pick up the pieces when Duncan broke her heart. But it felt so good to have someone on his side. And what was the harm, really? What was Hayden compared to him? Marlow was right. He and Birdie *did* have longevity on their side. And how could Hayden possibly love her more than he did, more than he had for as long as he could remember? He couldn't. No, Birdie was his; she just wouldn't admit it yet.

"The thing is, the thing about Birdie, is that she's like you," Duncan said slowly.

"She's fat too?"

He laughed. "No, she's tiny." He nudged her when she rolled her eyes. "She's a good girl, all deep and stuff. I annoy her greatly, me and my non-daydreaming shallowness. To her I'm just a jock. And," this part was hard for him to say, "she knows all my flaws, all of them. And they stand between us. It's hard for things not to feel hopeless." He sagged under the truth of his words. For so long he'd held out hope that he and Birdie would work out because they were meant to be. He still believed they were, but what if they didn't work out? Not everyone was guaranteed a happy ending.

"Hey," Marlow said sweetly, rubbing comforting little circle on his shoulder. "You're not so bad."

He laughed.

She shook his shoulder. "Not for me, obviously. I have higher standards. But for Birdie. You just need to show her something special, is all. Some part of you she's never seen before. You need to show her how much you've changed and matured in her absence, knock her off her feet like."

His lashes fluttered. She sounded so optimistic it made him feel the same. "How would I do that?"

"Well, this little nugget is a good start," she said, holding Darla aloft. "You're a good dad, an amazing dad. That's attractive. But you tell me, you know her better than I do."

He looked around as if searching for clues, but there was a pretty big one right in front of him. "This house. I bought it for her. I intended to fix it up for her, but..." he trailed off and shrugged. "I sort of lost heart."

Marlow reached for a piece of paper and pen from the stand to her right. In perfect teacher handwriting, she wrote, "HOUSE." "Good, what else?"

"She likes romance," he said. "She's girly that way, likes all those British movies, romantic comedies. She's a total sap."

"My kind of girl," Marlow mused, writing "ROMANCE" as he

spoke. She paused and touched the pen to her lips. "I've got an idea. Can you sing?"

He shook his head.

"I bet you can. Sing for me."

"What? Right now? I can't."

"Why not?"

"I don't know any songs."

"Everybody knows something. Sing 'Twinkle Twinkle Little Star.'"

"No."

She started to stand. He pulled her back and sang the stupid song. She considered him, tilting her head. "Not bad, I can work with that."

"What are you talking about?" he said, feeling nervous for the first time in recent memory.

"You're going to sing her a song at Sterling and Alby's reception."

Now he was the one to stand and start to walk away. She yanked him back. Blast, she was freakishly strong. "Are you trying to tell me you can pass a ball and make plays in front of a few hundred people, but singing one song to the woman you love scares you? Is him afwaid?" She stuck out her lip in an annoying pout.

He scowled. "No, but I don't know anything about singing. I'm an athlete, not a music guy."

"Lucky for you I'm both." She studied the list, tapping the pen. "Can you dance?"

"Of course."

She eyed him, dubious. "Let me see you."

"What? Now?"

"Do you require a stage and tap shoes?" She pressed a button on her laptop and music started. He swayed for her a few beats, getting into it, giving her the secret sauce.

She pressed her hand over her eyes. "Stop, I'm begging you. I wish I could unsee that."

"What? I'm an amazing dancer."

"No, you're an adequate swayer, you're a terrible dancer. You do that white guy thing of gyrating your hips, off rhythm, I might add."

"I was on the beat," he argued.

She shook her head.

"Women love how I dance."

"Women love how you look. They're too stupefied to look beyond the face," she said. "Or possibly just too stupid."

He jutted his finger at her. "I also have an amazing body."

"A body that doesn't know how to dance."

"And I suppose you're better at it," he said.

"It wouldn't take much, but yes, I actually *am* an amazing dancer."

"Prove it," he said.

She turned on some music, set Darla on the floor, and put her hands on his shoulders. "Pretend to be a post. It's all you're good for, at this point until I teach you."

Duncan was skeptical, but Marlow was incredible. Somehow she danced as if he were leading her when, really, all he did was stand still. She took his hand and twirled away, back, slid behind him, pressed her back to his front, rested his hand on her hip while she shimmied, her feet and hips doing miraculous things. It was, well, it was magical and more than a little alluring.

"Okay, that was, uh," he paused and cleared his throat. "That was pretty good." A lie, it was stinking amazing. "Where'd you learn to dance like that?"

"Ten years of lessons, plus I was a cheerleader."

"Pictures or it didn't happen," he said.

"No more pictures for you. I'm cutting off your addiction to thin me." She reached for the notebook and wrote "DANCING."

"Is that it? You want me to sing a song and do a dance? Easy peasy."

He watched her write something else. "NEVER SAY EASY PEASY AGAIN."

He barked a laugh and took the notebook out of her fingers, tossing it aside.

"There's one more thing," she said, turning serious. She took his hands in hers and held them, biting her lip as she gave him a pensive look. Suddenly it felt like the end of every date, and his heart gave a nervous kick.

"I already know how to kiss," he said.

"That's debatable, but not where I was going. I'm going to tell you a hard truth. Are you ready?"

He took a breath. "Bring it."

"You have to stop believing you own everyone in your world, that we are your personal chess pieces, to move around as you see fit," she said.

"It's not like that," he said scowling.

"But it is like that. Me, Darla, Sterling, and I'm going to guess Birdie fits that category. You view us as belonging to you."

"But you all do belong to me. You're my people," he said, pouting.

"Yes, but it's not pleasant the way you do it. It's manipulative and unhealthy. Sterling's allowed to have other friends and focus on his shop, I'm allowed to have a boyfriend and keep secrets, Darla is allowed to spend time with her mother, Birdie is allowed to take a job in the Mediterranean."

Now he was scowling and trying to tug his hands free but she held them in a vise. "Listen to me, you need to fix this. I'm telling you as a woman that we don't like it. If you want your relationship with Birdie to succeed, you need to pay attention."

"What am I supposed to do? Stop loving people? Stop talking to them? Wanting to spend time with them?"

"Stop believing that if you are not someone's sole focus it means they don't love you. I get it, you had your parents' undivided attention and adoration, you basked in it. But just because you don't have that with other people in your life doesn't mean they don't care deeply about you. Think about it this way. You can put a bird in a cage and make it your pet, or you can feed a bird at your window patiently day after day until it begins showing up on purpose. Which would be more meaningful? Which would be an act of love versus an act of servitude?"

"What if it doesn't show up? What if it goes away and never comes back?"

"You still have to let it go. Trying to make it stay, that won't ever work."

He blew out a breath, feeling suddenly exhausted. The thing was, he understood what she was trying to say. It was something he'd long realized about himself, the way he gripped everyone he loved so tightly. He hated feeling alone, feeling abandoned. "I bet you think this is because I'm adopted, huh?" he asked.

She smoothed the hair at his temple, a tenderly affectionate gesture that soothed him even more than her words. "I think it's because you're human and we all struggle with something. Relationships are hard. But I care enough to try to help you where you're struggling." She eased her arms around him and hugged, resting her head on his shoulder. It was…nice. She was soft, warm, and sturdy, not mushy like he'd first feared.

"You're way tall," he noted. She was only three inches shorter. That was kind of nice, too, not having to stoop to reach her, not feeling like she would break in his embrace.

"Don't be blurty," she chastised.

"Is there anything about me you like?" he asked, peeved.

"You give good hugs," she said.

"You should see what else I can…" she shoved away with a disgusted grunt. "What, you didn't even let me finish. I was going to say I also do the dishes," he called as she raced upstairs. He looked around for her laptop, but she'd taken it with her. Someday, he vowed, he would crack the mystery of what she was guarding so closely.

CHAPTER 11

To the surprise of neither Duncan nor Marlow, they didn't agree on what to do with the house. First Duncan didn't believe they could get it done before Birdie came home.

"Duncan, we're both perfectionists with a diehard work ethic. Do you really believe there's anything we can't do?" Marlow countered and, grinning, he'd finally agreed with her.

Next they had different ideas about paint.

"I want each room to be a different color," Duncan declared.

"That's nice, but no," Marlow said.

"You can't say no, it's my house."

"Hmm, that's odd because I'm pretty certain I just did. Let me try again: no."

"Why not?" he exclaimed.

"Because it's too piecemeal. You're going for continuity here. These rooms all open into each other with wide doorways. Ten different colors is way too schizophrenic."

"But Birdie likes color," he argued.

"And she will certainly get it. But not with paint."

He blinked, intrigued despite himself. "Then how?"

"Accents. Artwork, rugs, blankets. There will be plenty of color and plenty of texture."

"Do you promise?" he asked.

She pressed her hand to her chest in mock affront. "Do you honestly think I, Marlow, could possibly design something without charm and character when I ooze both of them in spades?"

"And you say I'm cocky," he complained, flicking her ponytail.

"But, see, I've earned mine. Yours is false bravado," she said.

"Fine, you can have the walls, but I'm painting the trim white."

She froze. "Say again."

"White trim," he said with an emphatic nod. "Looks so much cleaner and more modern."

"Why would you want to modernize a hundred and fifty year old house?" she asked.

"Why would you not? All this dark trim is depressing."

"It's walnut," she said.

"The most depressing nut," he said.

"You're the most depressing nut if you think I'm letting you paint this trim."

"Letting me? Good luck stopping me." He lunged for a paintbrush, intending to grab a can of paint and splash it on the living room trim before she could stop him, thereby sealing its fate, but he should have known better. Marlow leapt, tackling and taking him to the ground. They struggled wrestling back and forth until she eventually she pinned him, both arms over his head.

"Drop the brush," she demanded, enunciating each word.

"You can't watch me every minute," he said.

"I can break both your hands now, saving myself the trouble," she said, pressing hard on his palms.

"What do you have against white? Are you saying no to everything I want to be contrary?"

"Of course not. I'm saying no to white because it's the wrong choice. You're going for character. Nothing has more character than the original walnut."

"It's too dark," he yelled, suddenly furious. Why did she have to fight him on every blessed thing?

"Not after we paint the walls white," she yelled.

"I don't want white walls. I want white trim," he yelled.

"You're a big baby and you don't know what's good for you," she yelled.

"You tackle like a linebacker," he yelled.

"You fold like a house of cards," she yelled.

They stopped yelling because both of them seemed to realize they were sprawled on the floor, she fully on top of him, their faces a hairsbreadth apart, breathing hard. Duncan was seized with the sudden desire, no, *need*, to kiss her, and he wondered if she felt the same because she sat up abruptly and moved away, putting a few feet of distance between them. She took a breath.

"If I show you a mockup on my computer, will you please keep an open mind?" she asked.

He closed his eyes, trying to force away the strange images and yearnings now flowing through him. He took a few deep breaths, trying to get one that didn't have her in it. "Yes."

"Even if it takes a few minutes? You won't paint? Because that's permanent or at least a lot of work to undo."

"I won't paint," he promised. He didn't think he could move, not for a while, at least.

"Thank you," she said, sounding sweet and sincere when he wanted her to be cutting and sarcastic to make him forget the last few minutes. Or maybe he liked her sarcastic and cutting too. He shook his head. He must be really messed up and desperate since Birdie went away if the first woman he felt a spark of attraction to was Marlow, a woman completely off limits. They were friends, good friends, maybe best friends. But he couldn't see her that way. He couldn't sustain an attraction to her on any permanent basis, could he? Not with Birdie in the picture. And Birdie was still in the picture, would always be in the picture. He thought of her and his heart felt bruised and pulpy. When he thought of Marlow he felt...whatever the opposite of that was.

Mostly she made him laugh, when she wasn't making him angrier than all get out.

He lay on his back in silence a while, Marlow's clacking keyboard oddly soothing. She typed a lot and he had grown used to the sound, always knew where to find her in the house, based on the location of her tapping.

"Okay, you can look," she said eventually. He sat up and she scooted closer, shifting her computer onto his lap. He could tell she wanted to say stuff, to drive her point home, but she didn't. She merely let him look at the mockup design. Much as he hated to admit it, he loved it. Of course he couldn't let her win completely, though, so he gave a longsuffering sigh. "Fine, I'll let you win."

She snapped the laptop closed. "Liar. You never let me win, unless you already agree. We're like two bighorn sheep, butting heads at every possible opportunity."

"You love it," he accused.

She shrugged, smiling. They leaned against the couch and faced forward.

"Is this what it's like with him, your boyfriend?" he asked.

"No, but it's not supposed to be, is it? Jensen's sweet, sensitive, artistic. I'm pretty certain you're not supposed to want to kill the person you're with." She frowned and he matched her, both of them wondering why they liked arguing with each other so much if arguing wasn't supposed to be enjoyable.

"You're a strong personality," he said at last. "You'd have to be with someone sweet to balance you."

"And you," she said bringing her knees up and wrapping her arms around them. "I bet Birdie's sweet."

"Birdie's sweet," he agreed. "She doesn't let me get away with things, though. She calls me out, challenges me." He stared off into the distance, frowning. Birdie didn't have as much fight in her as he did. He could get her to give in, if he kept at her. They would bicker, and she would put up a struggle, but he would keep working on her until she caved. She had sass and a temper, but not as much stamina or perseverance as he did. That was how he knew they would eventually be together, because he would wear her down until she caved. But how would he feel after she caved? Satisfied because he'd gotten his way? Or disappointed because she hadn't?

"When are we going to get started on the house?" he asked, feeling antsy all of a sudden.

"How about now?"

"It's ten at night," he said.

She faced him with an eyebrow held aloft, challenge in every aspect of her features. "So?"

He smiled. "So we'd better get to the hardware store before they close at eleven." He stood and reached for her hand, tugging her up beside him. Sprinting now, hand in hand, they dashed for his car.

CHAPTER 12

"Ishould be paying you more," Duncan said. He and Marlow lay side by side on their backs, exhausted. Overhead, the ceiling was drying. Below, plastic drop cloths crinkled each time they so much as twitched. After arriving at the hardware store, they'd both miraculously agreed they should start with the ceilings. And now, in Darla's absence, they had painted every ceiling in the house. Duncan was a hard worker, but Marlow was a machine. He began to wonder if she was part robot; she didn't stop until the job was done.

"Definitely," Marlow agreed.

"Let's be clear, I won't. But I probably should," Duncan said. It was possible he had never been this physically exhausted. Who knew painting ceilings was such a workout? His shoulders ached something fierce, but he couldn't complain about it because Marlow had kept pace. Or possibly outworked him. As the project wore on, he found himself taking more and more breaks when she wasn't looking.

"It looks so good, though. I love it when everything looks all clean and fresh. Like snow."

"What would a Georgia girl like you know about snow?" he asked.

"There's this thing called TV. I'll show you sometime."

"How do you have the energy for sarcasm?"

"It's my lifeblood," she said. "I'm going to start working on replacing light fixtures next."

"I'll ask Sterling if he knows an electrician."

"Why? I can do it," she said.

"You know how to wire things?" he asked.

"You date a construction worker, you learn a few things."

"What kind of things?" he asked, nudging her.

"Nothing I'll ever show you. We need to plan a day to shop for artwork."

"What's wrong with the artwork I already have?" he asked, eyeing the posters he'd had since college.

"Please tell me you're joking," she said, tone scathing.

"...Sure."

She jabbed him and he winced. They lay in silence, staring at the ceiling some more, literally watching the paint dry.

"I hope...I hope she likes it," he said at last, uncharacteristically uncertain.

Marlow scooted closer, rested her head on his shoulder, clasped his hand, and gave it a squeeze. "She's going to love it."

He rested his head on hers with a sigh that felt a lot like contentment. A minute later, they were both asleep.

After that, their lives became segmented into With Darla and Without Darla. With Darla, they observed their normal routine, meaning life revolved around the baby and her schedule. On the evenings and weekends Without Darla, they worked like two people possessed, either on a house project or on Duncan himself.

After they finished painting the ceilings, they moved on to the walls, and then Marlow declared they needed to refinish the floors.

"I'll hire someone," Duncan said as he once again lay on the floor, exhausted from yet another marathon painting session. She was killing him, bit by bit. How had he ever thought her lazy, even for a moment?

"Why? It's not so hard. You rent a sander, apply new stain."

"There has to be more to it than that," he said.

"Nah," she said, waving him away. Seemingly nothing intimidated her, and he feared it as much as he respected it. Thanks to her, he now had new light fixtures in the entire downstairs, including a vintage crystal chandelier in the dining room she'd found at an estate sale. When she told him about it, he balked. He didn't want crystal in his dining room. But she insisted and, as usual, it was the perfect thing he didn't realize he needed.

"It still looks blah in here," he said. The walls were a pleasant shade of creamy white, and it was a nice contrast to the dark trim, but it still felt so empty.

"Ye of little faith." She sat up to stare down at him. Whenever she wanted to feel superior or gain the upper hand, she used height as her advantage, he realized. Her hair had come half undone from its messy bun and draped around her like a curtain, tickling his cheek. "I'm not done yet. The finishing touches are the best part."

Duncan wasn't certain about that. He thought this might be the best part, the working together to create something grand. No one but Sterling had ever come alongside him in such a fashion before. He smiled up at her and tucked a chunk of hair behind her ear. Birdie's hair was wiry and wild. Marlow's hair was silky and smooth.

"What?" she asked, eyeing his smile with suspicion.

"I'm enjoying the view," he said.

"I suppose that works both ways," she said, and now she was smiling as she reached out a hand to smooth his hair. "You sure are pretty, Duncan Shepherd."

"I thought you didn't like that about me," he said.

"Only when you try to make it be the sum total of who you are. But this hardworking boy, now there's a Duncan I can get on board with." She tossed him a little wink and lay down again.

"You're a flirt," he accused.

"Absolutely."

"And a tease."

"No."

"You are," he said, rolling toward her. "You promise all kinds of things you never deliver on."

She rolled to face him. "I state facts, I promise nothing. You have your Birdie, I have my Jensen. You and I are friends, the end."

He felt vaguely annoyed, and that annoyed him more. "You use Jensen as a shield because you're scared to get close to anyone."

"Nope."

"It's true. He's hours away, you've seen him once since you've been here, you barely talk about him."

She sat up again. "And you're the expert. At least there's not an ocean between me and mine."

He sat up. "That wasn't my choice. I wasn't the one who put an ocean between us. You're the one who moved away from yours."

"Because he didn't ask me to stay," she blurted, then looked like she wished she could take it back. She blinked furiously a few times, then stood and dashed from the room.

"No, wait, don't. I didn't mean it," Duncan called. The sound of her door slamming echoed through the house. With a sigh, he stood and went after her. He knocked a few times. "Marlow, come on. Hey."

"Go away."

"No." He tried the handle of her door and found it locked. "Open the door."

"No."

"Yes."

"No."

"Yes. You're being hardheaded. Open the door so we can talk."

She didn't answer.

"Open the door or I'll break it down," he threatened.

"No you won't, it's solid oak."

"What are you, part squirrel? How do you know every wood?" He was rewarded when she giggled. He knocked again, softly this time. "Come on. You said I needed to grow as a person. Do you know how often in my life I've tracked someone down to apologize?"

There was a shuffling sound and then she opened the door, poking her head around the edge. "How often?"

"One time, including this one." He reached out and touched her hair again, tenderly. "I'm sorry."

Her lip trembled and her eyes filled with tears. "I love him."

"I know you do."

"I want love to be enough."

He pulled her into a comforting hug. She rested her head on his shoulder. Her hair smelled good, like coconut, he thought absently. He rubbed a soothing little circle on her back. "Sometimes it is."

Her arms circled his waist and she let out a shuddery little sigh. "Sometimes it isn't. And then what?"

Duncan didn't answer because it was a question he'd asked himself, too, and he still didn't have an answer.

CHAPTER 13

"You're using the pads of your fingers," Marlow said.

"How can you tell when you're not looking?" Duncan complained.

"I have ears, don't I?" she said mildly.

With a huff of frustration, he resumed trying to make the correct chord on the guitar. He only had to learn three chords, but still it felt impossible. His fingers were clumsy and unaccustomed to the strange new contortions. Every night when Darla was home, and some nights when she wasn't, he picked up Marlow's guitar and practiced, ostensibly to learn the song but also because it was as soothing to play as it was to listen. Duncan didn't think of himself as a nervous person, but even so he could feel the tension and anxiety drain from him whenever the guitar was near. "What are you doing?" he asked after being unable to figure it out from staring.

"Knitting a blanket," she explained.

"Don't you need needles for that?" he asked. His grandma knit; he knew the signs.

"This is hand knitting. It makes those big chunky blankets like the one I made for Darla's room."

"I didn't know you made that," he said, impressed. "You can do all the things."

"Yes," she agreed, and he laughed.

"What's this one for? My room?"

She grimaced. "I'm not making you an afghan. That's too girl-friendy. This is for the couch."

"It's going to look stellar on Grammy's orange nightmare," Duncan replied. The couch came with the house, another thing he'd been meaning to update.

"Now seems like a good time to tell you I bought you a new couch," Marlow said in the same casual tone.

Duncan looked up from the guitar. "What?"

"It's green velvet, totally retro cool, you'll love it."

"How much did it set me back, or am I allowed to know?"

"*Three thousand,*" she mouthed.

He sighed and resumed plucking. "You're going to drive me straight to the poorhouse."

"Nah, I saw your bank statement lying on the counter the other day. You're fine."

He tossed her a wink. "That's what all the girls say."

She laughed, intent on her knitting. "Oh, before I forget to tell you, I'm going to Savannah next weekend."

He stopped playing. "What? Why?"

"Visiting Jensen. As you rightfully pointed out, I'm a bit overdue."

"What am I supposed to do?" he asked, tone petulant.

"Practice," she said.

He frowned, thinking. "I'll go with you."

"That's sweet, but I think Jensen might eventually object to your continued presence," she said.

Duncan didn't think so, but he knew better than to say it out loud. "Not like that. I have a buddy who lives in Savannah and has been bugging me to visit. I should probably take advantage of these rare weekends of no baby before my twenties end. Sterling keeps warning me once we reach thirty we have to be real grownups."

"You really don't mind giving me a ride?" she asked. It would be way more comfortable to ride in his Audi than her mess of a jalopy.

"Nope, we'll split gas."

She nodded. He reached out a foot and kicked her. "I'm joking, dunce cap. Of course you have to pay for all the gas, it's your trip."

"You think you're so funny," she said, eyeing him as he remained grinning at her.

"I do," he agreed, supremely cocky until he badly botched a chord and had to start again.

"Maybe you'd better stay home and practice," she said.

"It's no good to practice when you're not here because I don't know if I'm doing it wrong, and I certainly can't practice dancing without you."

"You don't practice dancing with me," she accused.

He was strangely averse to learning to dance with her, and he didn't know why. But she was right, if he didn't learn with her, he wouldn't be able to do it with Birdie. "Fine." He set the guitar aside. "Let's do it now."

"Wait, I have to extract myself," she said, drowning in a sea of over-sized white yarn.

"You look like a spider's next meal," he said.

She fished herself out of the yarn and set it aside. She stood and faced him, placing her hands on his shoulders. "Okay, those hip gyrations."

"Are smooth," he inserted.

"Maybe for the club, but this is romance, this is wooing. You don't lead with your hips, you lead with your confidence, you show her what you've got. The dance floor is your domain, you're completely in charge."

"Finally," he said.

She put her hand in his and gave a little curtsy. "I surrender myself to you. You tell me where to go and bring me back again."

The music started, and it was easier than he thought it would be, likely because Marlow already knew what she was doing so it only seemed like he was in charge. But he liked the feeling of leading her, of taking her where he wanted to go.

In the middle of their second successful dance, the electricity flicked off. They froze. "Now what?" he muttered.

"Keep going."

"There's no music," he said.

She started to sing while they swayed. He loved to hear her sing, her voice low and mellow. He cinched her closer, his hand easing around her waist. She had a waistline, he noted, an exaggerated hourglass. The moon streaming through the window was their only light. Marlow sang and they swayed and it was one of those perfect moments, the one your mind flicks to when it's trying to conjure something good.

He wondered if Marlow felt the same because she shifted, removing her hand from his grasp to slide her arms around his neck. Duncan rested both hands on her waist, easing her impossibly closer. They swayed together, locked in some kind of ancient dance rhythm they both seemed to know by instinct. At some point she stopped singing so the sound of their mingled, strained breathing was the only noise in the room. His cheek brushed hers, his stubble scraping her impossibly soft skin. His nose nudged her, asking her without words to turn her head, to tip her lips toward his. Her breathing hitched as her head slowly rose, lips parted.

The lights flicked on.

They froze, blinking at each other in startled confusion, mere centimeters apart, neither daring to breath. Marlow was the first to take a step back and draw a deep breath. "You're really coming along," she said, the words tumbling upon each other like runoff.

"I have a good teacher," he said, fingers flexing at his sides, fighting the urge to reach, to touch.

She ripped her gaze away and turned toward the stairs. "I think I hear my phone. I should…" Her head nudged toward the stairs.

"Sure," he said, taking a step back as if releasing her.

She sagged slightly as if some sort of physical restraint had been broken and then dashed away, skittering up the stairs two at a time.

"What was that?" Duncan whispered to himself as he sank to the couch. He put his head in his hands. Her computer caught his eye in his peripheral. She never left it out, never left it unguarded. It was only because they'd come so close to losing their minds that she left it here just now.

He reached for it, shamelessly intent on snooping. What was she doing with this thing, her near constant companion? A file was already open. He heard her moving around upstairs. She could return at any time. Quickly he logged into his email, sent himself the file, and logged back out again.

By the time she returned, he was once again plucking the guitar, staring into space, the picture of innocence. Her eyes landed on her laptop with alarm, shifted to him, then back to her computer. His heart thundered as she opened it and clicked a few things, but then she seemed to relax.

I'm too good at sneaking to get caught, he assured himself, repressing a smile as he continued to strum.

Except maybe he wasn't because an odd sort of tension lingered between them, growing as the minutes passed. Duncan felt it, and he was certain Marlow did, too. She kept tossing him little looks when she thought he didn't notice, but of course he noticed because he was tossing her looks, too. Where was Darla as a buffer when they needed her? Her weekends with Chelsea would be his undoing, in more ways than one.

At last Marlow set aside her knitting and took a deep breath, as if bracing for something. "I think we need to talk."

"Do we?" he said, aiming for that jerk guy thing, pretending to be oblivious to the simmering tension. Why did women feel the need to trot everything out and beat it to death? So they'd had an almost moment, no biggie. They lived in the same house; it was bound to happen occasionally.

"Yes." She fidgeted, nervous. He watched as she reached for her knitting, set it down, picked it up again and then stared at it. "The thing is."

He braced himself, prepared to let her down easy. *You and I are friends. I'm not interested in you that way. I have Birdie, remember?* He would be gentle, more gentle than he'd ever been because this was Marlow and she was so special to him. Maybe he'd tell her that. Women loved that kind of stuff, ate it up.

"I think we should do the kitchen."

He drew his gaze off the far wall and landed it on her. "What?"

"The kitchen. I know we said we weren't going to because we didn't have time, but we're almost done with the other stuff. If we hurry we can do it."

"The kitchen," he repeated, still trying to pull his mind back from where it had gone. "You want to do the kitchen."

She nodded, scooting forward in earnest supplication. She reached out a hand and rested it on his forearm. "I'm totally optimistic we can get it done. We can get this entire house finished before your Birdie gets home. Wouldn't that be something?"

"Something," he repeated dully.

Satisfied, she sat back with a smile and picked up her knitting. "We agreed on something without coming to blows. Wonders never cease."

He nodded, feeling vague and out of it, sort of like the last time he had the stomach flu. He woke on the third day, his mind a muddle of weakness and low blood sugar. Happy now, she resumed knitting and he began plucking on the guitar, the gentle melody the only sound in the room until at last he sat up straight and looked at her.

"What? I don't want do the kitchen. There is no way we can get it done, we shouldn't even start."

She tossed aside her knitting. "You are such a wancy. We can totally get it done."

"Who's going to do it, you?"

"Who else?"

He reached for a pillow and tossed it at her, ducking when she threw one in return. *Finally back to normal,* he thought, breathing a sigh of relief. He could almost swear she breathed one, too.

CHAPTER 14

On Friday, Marlow only had a half-day of work. Chelsea took off early for some family plans, which would allow Marlow time to finish a few house projects before she and Duncan left for Savannah. Or that was the plan until Duncan showed up exactly as Chelsea arrived.

"Hey, what are you doing home so soon?" she greeted him.

"Chelsea texted me she was taking off early, so I thought I would too. We can get a jump start on Savannah, not have to pull in so late," he said.

She remained staring at him, feeling a sudden premonition that maybe she shouldn't go to Savannah. Maybe it was better if she didn't see Jensen.

"What?" he asked.

She jumped to attention. "Nothing. You're right, this is better, thanks." Her eyes bounced between him and Chelsea, wondering anew over their complete lack of relationship. They didn't hate each other, per se, but there was certainly no love lost between them, which was kind of odd because they were both spectacularly nice looking. In Marlow's experience, like tended to attract like. In this case it seemed to repel. When Duncan still failed to acknowledge the mother of his child, Marlow filled the void, stepping forward to give her a hug.

"Have fun this weekend. I hope you get a chance to rest and relax."

"You too," Chelsea said, returning her hug. "I want details on Monday, let me know if Jensen finally got his hair cut."

They shared a laugh, one that could only be accomplished by inside jokes. Duncan crossed his arms over his chest, watching them with a curious scowl.

"Duncan," Chelsea said at last, coolly.

"Chelsea," he replied in the same cool tone, then reached for the baby when she lunged at him, kissing her cheeks and beaming when she began to laugh.

"I didn't know you and Chelsea were friends," he noted when she and the baby were finally gone.

"Of course we are. We see each other practically every day," Marlow said.

"Yeah, but she's so…meh. It's like talking to a wet dishrag. I couldn't stand her when she was with Sterling, I can barely stomach her now."

"Sounds like true love," Marlow said. She was goading him, he could tell, but he couldn't help but react.

"What? No."

"Come on, you know how it is. Two people who hate each other *always* secretly love each other. All that passion." She wagged her brows.

"Chelsea and I don't fight, and we don't hate each other. We tolerate each other grudgingly for the baby's sake. Blech." He shuddered.

"Hey," she said seriously, reaching out to lay a hand on his forearm. "That's your baby's mama. Y'all are going to be connected for the next eighteen years, like family."

"I'm trying," he said, tone defensive. "I don't know what it is about her, but she rubs me the wrong way."

"I know exactly what it is," she said.

"Do not say I'm secretly in love with her," he said, grimacing.

"No, it's that she exists. You want Darla all to yourself, just like you wanted Sterling all to yourself. You resent Chelsea because she is or was in between you and those things."

He opened his mouth to protest, thought better of it, and scowled at her. "Then why doesn't she like me? For the same reason?"

"No, because she says you're a self-centered egotistical jerk."

His scowl morphed to a smile. "At least she's observant. How much longer is it going to take you to get ready?"

"I have to get presentable," she said, giving a self-conscious little touch to her messy bun.

"You have exactly until I finish packing," he warned.

She rolled her eyes, knowing he was bluffing without saying the words. He didn't argue because she was right, he wouldn't actually do anything. There was no point in leaving without her. But with Marlow, he could never resist throwing out a challenge or staking his territory.

They walked upstairs together and separated, he to his room and she to her bathroom. As he predicted, he was ready to go first. Bored and restless, he stood in the doorway of her bathroom, watching her primp.

He didn't know a lot about women's makeup, but she seemed to have particular skill, could transform her face from pretty to sublime with the flick of a few tools. In the beginning he resented that she only dressed up for other people, but now he found it comforting. Others might get the perfectly painted visage, but he got the real Marlow, flaws and all. Though he had yet to find any flaws. Her complexion was perfect, her eyes an arresting shade of blue-green. Her lashes were long but so lightly colored that, without mascara, it was hard to see them unless you were up close. He saw them a lot, he realized. Every day, in fact. They were nearly always together, always side by side, within touching distance if either of them were so inclined to reach out a hand. Neither of them was, curiously. They inhabited the same space every day, day after day, and yet they pivoted and orbited around each other like two tiny planets, their courses already set and determined, too risky to deviate and change.

What would happen if I touched her? Unable to contain his curiosity, he reached out a hand and slid it beneath her hair, squeezing the back of her neck. Her eyes darted to his, startled, inquisitive.

"Nervous?" he asked.

She took a shaky breath. "A little." She faced the mirror and put on some shiny lip gloss. "I don't know why I did that. I'm going to have to do it again in a few hours when we get there."

"Maybe you secretly want to look good for me," he tried.

She gave him a little smile and shook her head. "Pointless."

"Not pointless. I appreciate beauty in all its forms."

"I am begging you to stop talking."

"You take everything the wrong way," he accused.

"How is 'I appreciate beauty in all its forms' a compliment?"

"How is it not? It's me telling you you're beautiful," he said.

"No, it's you adding a qualifier. When you see something beautiful, like an amazing sunset or painting, you say, 'It's so beautiful.' When you see something and you're able to find the beauty, despite how repulsive it is, for instance a coral snake or deadly jellyfish, you say, 'I appreciate beauty in all its forms.' See the difference?"

She was right. As hard as he had tried lately not to take her size into account, he still did. Anytime he looked at her and thought she was beautiful, which was every time he looked at her, his brain always added a silent, *for a fat girl.* Despite how hard he was trying to overcome his prejudice, it was still there. And he hated it. "I'm sorry," he said sincerely, and he was. He wanted to be that guy who could look at her and see *her*, regardless of size. She made him want to be that guy, and it bothered him that he wasn't. A lot.

She gave him a heart achingly sad little smile. "Cheer up, you're not alone. I can read it in a guy's expression. They look at my face and think, 'Wow,' then look at the rest of me and think, 'Oh.' Dismissal, in an instant."

"But not Jensen," he said, aiming to regain their earlier good cheer.

She smiled, allowing the moment to pass, allowing the mood to lighten. "Speaking of, I should text and let him know I'll be early."

"Or you could surprise him," he said, poking her bicep. "Guys like that kind of thing. Keeps the spark alive."

"I suppose we could do with a few more sparks," she said, linking her arm with his.

The trip to Savannah was fun, their earlier serious moment forgotten. "You didn't tell me he lives in the historic neighborhood," Duncan accused.

"To be fair, I haven't actually told you anything about him. Plus it's Savannah. Pretty much all of it is the historic neighborhood. You can drop me here."

"I don't get to see inside?" he said, full sadness.

"You're a big baby," she said, but he knew that was his entrée. He walked slowly behind her, pausing to stare at bricks or cornices or anything else that caught his interest on the old house. Marlow ascended the porch steps and reached for the door. It was old and warped, the latch never sticking properly unless you got aggressive and gave it a slam. It was partially open now and she froze, remembering all the times she let herself in, as if she belonged, as if there were no space between her and Jensen. Could she do that now? *Should* she do that now? She was still his girlfriend.

Taking a breath for courage, she pushed open the door, took a step inside, and froze. Jensen lay on the couch, a girl in his arms, their bodies tangled together, lips locked in a frenzied kiss. Duncan came up behind her and it was he who made the pained little sound of surprise that finally caught their attention. Jensen looked up and locked eyes with Marlow in one of those horrible moments that seems to linger an inordinate amount of time, but in reality probably only lasted a few seconds.

She turned and walked back out of the house, Duncan keeping pace beside her this time. "Marlow, wait," Jensen called. She could hear him scrambling to untangle himself from the girl, and the mental image of that hurt an unbelievable amount.

Thanks to their long strides, she and Duncan reached the car before Jensen reached them. Duncan put it in reverse and made a satisfying squeal as they peeled away. He didn't talk, and she was thankful. She stared out the window, the numbness of shock giving way to physical pain. So this was how people died of a broken heart because, at the moment, she genuinely felt like she might perish from the deep ache now rocking her midsection. Jensen wasn't perfect, but she had always thought him good, had always believed him above reproach, had placed him above other men, men like Duncan who got his best friend's girlfriend pregnant on a whim. And now this man she loved, had trusted, had cheated on her. Had he always cheated on her and she'd been too blind to realize? Could anyone be trusted? Was anyone good?

Duncan handed her a bag and she realized he had driven through a fast food restaurant. He must be starved. Poor guy. "You should eat something," he urged.

She took the bag, but she wasn't hungry. Suddenly she remembered his reason for coming to Savannah. "Drop me at a hotel somewhere and go see your friend." She gave his arm a squeeze and tried to smile, turning toward the window again when it wobbled precariously, an unconvincing lie.

Duncan didn't reply, but a few minutes later they arrived in front of a swanky hotel, far outside of Marlow's budget. *Who cares?* She thought. Who cared that she was likely about to spend a week's salary for a night? What was the point of saving money anymore? She had been saving for a future that no longer existed, marriage, motherhood. She might as well spend it all now, enjoy herself and have fun while she at least had youth on her side.

She ambled toward the hotel's entrance, but Duncan whistled for her, hailing her back. Normally she would have been annoyed at being summoned like a pooch, but now she didn't care. She watched vaguely as he unloaded her luggage from the trunk. She shouldered it, and then he retrieved his own luggage.

"What are you doing?"

"Come on," he said, in lieu of an answer. He led the way into the hotel and toward an elevator.

"I have to check in," she said. It had been a long time since she stayed at a hotel, but she was still familiar with the process.

"I did virtual check in," he said.

"What about a key?"

"You're delightfully old fashioned," Duncan replied, tossing her a smile.

She didn't respond, and his smile morphed to a frown.

They arrived at what was apparently the correct floor and he held up his phone. The door unlocked and he pushed it open.

"That's fancy," she couldn't help but mutter, and he laughed.

He held the door for her. She eased inside and couldn't help but be awed by the room, much better than any other place she'd stayed. On vacation, her parents tended to get the cheapest room possible, usually a highway motel. This suite looked presidential with granite, two TVs, plush linens. Everything seemed to sparkle. "Wow, this is so nice. Have you stayed here before?"

"Every time I come to Savannah," he said, blasé. He traveled a lot for his job, likely stayed in lots of places like this. He certainly held none of the awe Marlow did. She realized she was still holding her bag of food. The smell of stale oil was already starting to mar the scent of cultivated wealth in the room. She set down her luggage but retained her purse.

"I should go get my own room," she said, turning toward the door.

"Nope," he said in his best "don't argue with me because I know everything" tone. It usually made her bristle, and today was no exception, except her hackles didn't rise as much as usual.

"I can't take your room," she said.

"You won't. We'll share it."

"There's only one bed," she noted.

He laughed and plopped onto it, reaching for the remote.

She blinked at him. "What are you doing?"

"Watching TV."

"What about your friend?" she asked.

"I already texted him and canceled, told him something came up."

"You can't do that," she said.

"Why not?"

"Because he's your friend and you had plans."

He muted the TV. "Marlow, I don't care about him. He's not my inner circle. You are. I'm not leaving you alone after that."

Just like that the dam broke and she burst into tears, letting her purse drop as she covered her face with her hands. Duncan stood and gathered her close, holding her in a comforting hug as she cried. When it became clear the tears wouldn't stop anytime soon, he herded her to the bed and gave her a little shove. She lay down and curled into a ball. Duncan eased in beside her, the solid weight of his arm over her middle like an anchor. She curled into him, unfurling her pain and pressing it into his care. It felt so good to let go and lean on him, better than anything in recent memory.

She cried until she was all cried out, until she cried herself to sleep, still curled into Duncan's comforting embrace.

Not having any sisters or close girl cousins, Duncan had never been privy to a woman's tears when he wasn't the one who caused them. Girls had cried at him, of course, because of some action on his part. But he hadn't cared about their tears because he hadn't cared about them. But he cared about Marlow, cared deeply, and seeing her in so much pain brought an echoing spasm of pain in his own heart. It hurt, physically hurt to see her weep so wrenchingly, especially because he knew it wasn't her norm. She wasn't the sort of girl given easily to tears. She was strong, tough, capable. And now she was so close to broken it scared him.

Was this what it was like for Birdie? He knew he hurt her with the announcement of Chelsea's pregnancy, but he had brushed her pain aside because he hadn't directly cheated on her. He and Birdie weren't together when he had his thing with Chelsea. Therefore it shouldn't have hurt her. But it did, and he suddenly realized she had probably cried this way, that he had caused her this sort of heart wrenching pain, and how could he stand it?

Women weren't like men, he realized now. He had been hurt before, lots of times, but not like this. Not a searing pain that seemed to touch his soul and shred his heart. How could they stand to face the world with that soft little thing fluttering in their chest, so vulnerable, so prone to being broken and ruined by men? No wonder some women became hard, no wonder some women hated men. Their tender little hearts had likely been wounded beyond recovery.

And he'd been one to wound. He had only ever loved Birdie, therefore other women hadn't mattered to him. He had used them and tossed them away, wrongly believing they wouldn't be affected because *he* hadn't been affected. For his sake, he hoped karma wasn't real. If so, he had a lot of comeuppance in his future. And then a new horror struck him: Darla. Would he have to watch his payback play out in the form of his sweet, innocent baby daughter? Would some man eviscerate her heart this way? He wanted to find the guy and commit a preemptive murder. Short of that, he wanted to go back in time and be a better man, a better example of what a man should be for his daughter.

Duncan always believed he would be different with Birdie, that he would never treat her the way he treated other women. And he hadn't, but he had broken her heart nonetheless. Was there something fundamentally wrong with him as a man? Or were all men this prone to villainy? Marlow had set Jensen on a pedestal, and Duncan had come to think of him that way, too, had been glad for her sake she had someone so good. But now he'd been knocked off the pedestal in the worst possible way. Was no one worthy?

Sterling is good, he remembered. Sterling had tried hard never to wound, had been careful with girls' hearts. Maybe because he had a sister and better understood the repercussions, or maybe because he was merely a better man. Whatever the reason, Sterling was everything he seemed to be—mature, responsible, conscientious.

Without disturbing Marlow, Duncan reached for his phone and texted him now.

Please never cheat on Alby.

WHAT? Sterling replied.

I just...need to believe you're the real deal.

Alby's my heart. I'd have to throw away my own heart to hurt her, Sterling replied, and Duncan smiled, relieved.

Good. I'll be watching, he added, in case Sterling ever got any ideas or temptations. Duncan decided he would never be that best friend who covered for lies and made excuses for bad behavior. He would be the sort of best friend who held Sterling to a higher standard, who constantly ensured he was the sort of man he was supposed to be. It was what Sterling did for him, what Marlow did for him, made him want to be better.

Thanks. It was such a Sterling thing to say that Duncan almost laughed. "Thanks," wouldn't have been his usual reply. Previously he would probably have chafed at the oversight. But now he got it, now he understood. Being excellent was hard work. It took a village.

Are you okay? Sterling asked a minute later.

I... His glance slid to Marlow. Her secrets weren't his secrets to tell. *Marlow's having a bad time, and I wish I were better equipped to help. Could use some Sterling magic right now.* Sterling always knew the right thing to say, the right thing to do. It was why, despite Duncan's devastating good looks, girls had always preferred Sterling to him.

You have Duncan magic. Marlow is yours, not mine. You know what to do.

She's not mine, he started to type and then erased it. He set his phone aside and reached for her, sliding his arm around her and rubbing a little circle on her back. She snuggled closer and gripped his shirt in one hand, balling it as she gave a shuddery little sigh. Her eyes were swollen from crying, her face blotchy and red, but it did nothing to detract from her beauty. It was as if now that he'd seen it, he could never unsee it, no matter how she looked. He eased his hand up and pushed the hairs away from her face, unsticking them from her wet cheeks. She slept the sleep of the heartbroken, undisturbed by his touch. He pressed a kiss to her forehead, and it felt strangely like placing a seal upon her. *Mine.* She was under his care now, under his protection, this woman who gave so much of herself caring for him and his daughter. She made him laugh, she made him crazy, but she was irrevocably a part of him in some way now, and it bothered him greatly to see her so wounded. Feeling like a knight of old, he vowed that he would do whatever possible to bring her back again, to make her whole.

Something within him felt settled, all the way down to his soul. He continued to stare at her, his blinks becoming heavier, until he slipped into a deep and dreamless sleep.

CHAPTER 15

In the morning Marlow woke curled into a self-protective ball, eyes nearly swollen shut. Worse, she was pressed firmly against Duncan's chest, as if siphoning silent support in her sleep. And he had apparently been bestowing it if his arm over her waist was any indication. Before last night's heartache returned, she felt only mortification. That Duncan saw her that way, so pathetic and broken, was almost worse than the heartbreak. She, who prided herself on her strength, had been reduced to a miserable ball of weeping. It shamed her, that display of utter brokenness. And yet she had faith he wouldn't hold it against her. Still, it felt like allowing him the upper hand in a way she didn't understand. She had been cheated on by her boyfriend of four years, of course it was reasonable she should cry, should feel pain. But falling apart that way in front of Duncan…it left her feeling vulnerable in a way that was worse than anything else.

No more, she vowed, staring at his ridiculously handsome face, made more boyish in sleep. His mouth was slightly ajar and he snored softly. Not enough to be annoying, just enough to convince someone he wasn't actually perfect, might have a few flaws if anyone chose to look beyond the flawless exterior. Marlow had grown so used to him as a person, she hardly saw the exterior anymore. Occasionally, like now, she would be struck anew by the impossible faultlessness of his features. How was it possible that one person could be so classically handsome? She wished he weren't, wished he had a too-big nose or massively receding hairline or some other blemish that might have made him have to work harder to be loved. Instead all he had to do was show up, flash his megawatt smile, and life was handed to him on a platter. Except the mysterious Birdie. Already Marlow liked her for holding out on him. What would happen, she wondered, when Birdie gave in to him? And she would, Marlow had no doubts. Because once someone looked beyond the surface, maybe deep beyond, Duncan had a lot going on. He was successful, wealthy, a homeowner, funny, intelligent, an amazing father. The things that had made him so unattractive in the beginning, the selfishness and immaturity, were slowly being replaced and refined. Duncan Shepherd was growing up. Miss Birdie Thompson was going to be blown away.

And where did that leave Marlow?

You've never figured into the equation, she reminded herself. She and Duncan were friends, yes. But they weren't the sort of friends who could sustain him being in a serious relationship. She was a placeholder for the woman he actually wanted, the one who would likely wear a size four wedding dress.

Maybe Marlow could take Birdie's place and go to the Mediterranean. They could switch roles, like in *The Parent Trap*. Birdie would stay home and care for Duncan and Darla; Marlow would live her best life in Italy. What were the chances she could convince Birdie to throw her Mediterranean boyfriend into the deal? Marlow hadn't seen a picture of him, but she'd bet he was hot. Mediterranean boyfriends always were, somehow.

She eased from under Duncan's arm and closed herself into the bathroom, not daring to look into the mirror. She knew what she would find—hair a mass of tangles, eyes nearly swollen shut, face red and blotchy. *Not today, Satan.* She would put herself together, would look as good as humanly possible, for Duncan. Maybe it was conceited to think she could use her appearance as a thank you when he had made it clear many times he saw her as nothing but a fat girl, but at the moment it was all she had. He had commented a few times that she always dressed up for other people; today she would dress up for him. At the very least she could be that quintessential fat girl, the one with the pretty face. Resolved, she turned the shower on full blast and stepped beneath the spray.

When Duncan woke, he was groggy and disoriented, almost like days of old, pre-Darla, when he was hungover. Why did he feel so… odd? So empty and peculiar. He sat up and looked around. Hotel room, check. Savannah, check. Marlow. Marlow? Where was Marlow? He felt panicked for a few seconds, thinking maybe she had run away, before coming back to his senses. Marlow would never run from anything. Not a fight, not a man, not heartbreak. Nothing but him that first day, because she thought he was a serial killer. He smiled at the memory, remembering how he'd tackled her and she'd fought him. *She would have made an amazing quarterback,* he thought absently, smile widening.

The bathroom door opened and it was like a scene from a movie as Marlow emerged, backlit by the bathroom light. Duncan could swear her hair moved, as if there were a fan on her. She was so beautiful he almost had to squint to see her proper, had to discipline himself not to reach up, rub his eyes, and do an exaggerated double take.

She perched beside him on the edge of the bed and smiled, perfect mouth curving over perfect teeth. He stared at her perfect lips as they formed words and spoke.

"What have you got going on today?"

She sounded so normal, but then he knew she would. She would not be happy about her breakdown last night, was probably already plotting how to regain face. Her appearance this morning was an astonishing beginning. She had asked him a question. How long ago? Words, what were the words he was supposed to say now? "Not a thing," he croaked and hoped she chalked the croakiness up to early morning and not the speechlessness of having her perfection so nearby. She had never dressed up for him this way before, he realized, never turned the full power of her beauty on him. But what if it wasn't for him? What if she was meeting with Jensen? Feeling suddenly jealous, his brows lowered to a frown. "What do you have going on today?"

She leaned forward slightly, resting her palms on the bed. Her luxurious hair tumbled off her shoulders, swaying gently beside her face, drawing his attention back to her mouth. "I thought maybe we could spend the day looking for some artwork, for the house. If that's okay?"

Her big, blue-green eyes blinked at him once, twice, three times, awaiting his answer. Once when he was five his parents took him to Disney. He met Cinderella in person and got her autograph and his reaction to her had been the same as it was now. He nodded, mute. He would probably say yes to anything she asked at this point. He could only hope she would ask a lot more.

"What does Birdie like?"

The mention of Birdie was like a bucket of cold water to his head and heart. Birdie, right. That was what all of this was for. He cleared his throat and tried to think straight, hard to do when every breath brought a fresh whiff of Marlow. He closed his eyes, trying to envision Birdie's wiry brown hair, but it kept getting replaced with Marlow's silky strands. "Birdie likes things with meaning, things that are homemade, not modern art, never that. Homespun, simple." There. He opened his eyes and found her smiling affectionately at him.

"What a coincidence, me too. I think your Birdie and I have a lot in common. We're going to get along fine."

"Birdie gets along with everybody," he said. He couldn't think of one person Birdie had ever disliked.

"Maybe she can give me some pointers," Marlow said.

"Nah, you do all right," he said softly. She was good with people. He knew because *he* was good with people, when he wanted to be. It was what made him a good salesman. "Have you ever considered sales?"

"Maybe I will. I'll likely be out of a job soon."

He sat up. "What? Why?"

"Uh, because you'll hopefully be in a relationship with Birdie, one that will likely end in marriage. She'll want to find someone who agrees with her."

"But I want you," he blurted.

She laughed and reached out, smoothing a messy portion of his hair. "Thanks for the vote of confidence. I'm going to wrangle us some coffee while you shower. Something tells me this place has the good stuff."

"They do. Tell them Duncan sent you." He brushed his thumb on her cheek. It was only fair, she'd touched him first.

She laughed, a well-practiced flirtatious sound. "And what will that get me?"

"A whole lot of trouble, probably," he said, his deep thoughts from the night before still too close to the surface.

She leaned forward and kissed his cheek, pausing to whisper in his ear, "Some trouble is worth it."

When she walked out of the room, he was still staring after her, dazed.

He was used to women flirting with him, hitting on him. He had come to take it for granted. So he knew for a fact that Marlow was good at it, really good at it. Just now she had been putting on a front, trying to redeem herself after the humiliation of last night. But someday she would turn that charm on someone for real, would bend a man into a pretzel, would make him desperate to be with her. And how would that feel, to stand by and watch all that wit and strength, talent and beauty bestowed on some other man?

Like a kick in the teeth. Birdie or no Birdie, Duncan didn't think he would be able to stomach it. Though she would probably be long gone by the time she was ready to move on from Jensen. She was right, if he and Birdie were together, she wouldn't, *couldn't* stay. She would go somewhere else, find another man, hopefully one more worthy of her. Everything would be as it should. Why then did the thought hurt so much?

This was why he refused to be introspective. It brought nothing but pain. He slid out of bed and headed toward the bathroom, trying to push away every last thought.

CHAPTER 16

Savannah with Marlow was a blast, but then everything was Marlow was fun. She embraced absolutely everything with an optimistic sense of adventure that was uplifting by proximity. A sudden flash of insight told him she would always be thus, would be that old woman who made aging seem fun. She would never lose her sparkle, wit, or sense of humor. *What an odd thought to have,* Duncan mused, giving his head a little shake. But as much as he tried to dislodge it, it was a thought that settled deep, burrowing inside him like a chigger. The only other woman he'd ever considered such things about was Birdie. Birdie would always be sweet and quirky, the type to wear a different fancy hat every day and name the squirrels at her feeder.

I am losing my mind. Was this what fatherhood had done to him? Made him ponder old women? Or was it that he was beginning to realize he would likewise one day be old, and what type of woman did he want by his side? Certainly none of the women he'd dated. He couldn't picture any of them old, mostly because they had all been the sort to live for today—fast, hard, cheap. Until this moment he hadn't realized how interchangeable they all had been. Without exception, every one of them had been almost embarrassingly impressed by his car, his job, his face, his body. None of them had ever told him his hips gyrated like a drunk monkey when he danced or that he was spoiled and entitled, too used to getting what he wanted too easily. None but Marlow, who had said those things and then some. But instead of insults, it was as if she meant them for his benefit, the same way he had felt compelled last night to let Sterling know he'd be watching him. Because he loved him enough to always want him to be the best sort of man. That was the same way Marlow had said those things to him, because she cared enough to want him to be better. None of the other women had cared if he was spoiled, shallow, selfish. Most likely because they had been those things, too.

It took bravery to tell someone the painful truths they needed to hear. Birdie had done it, too, before she left. She had told him she hoped he got himself together and grew up because he had a lot to give. He hadn't been ready to hear it then; he was ready to hear it now.

"Marlow."

A woman spoke from nearby. Marlow and Duncan turned to her together. She was an older woman, not quite his mom's age, but almost, artsy and bohemian in the extreme with layers of mismatched clothing and scarves. Duncan wondered if it was her studio they were currently strolling.

"Avril," Marlow said, reaching forward to hug the woman.

"I thought you moved away," Avril said, darting Duncan a curious glance.

"I did, but I came back for a visit."

"Are you and Jensen still together?"

Marlow swallowed hard and forced a smile. "No, we're not."

Avril's eyes once again landed on Duncan, making a curious inspection. With no idea why, Duncan took Marlow's hand and wove their fingers together, giving them a squeeze. She returned the squeeze and her smile looked less strained. "This is Duncan," she said, leaving the other woman to puzzle their connection. "We're looking for some artwork for his house, a knockout nineteenth century farmhouse. I remember you used to have an artist who did some primitives, Grandma Moses type stuff."

Avril perked up, her earlier curiosity forgotten in light of a possible sale. "Yes, around this corner. Follow me." She led them to a far, forgotten corner with multiple paintings on display. "To be honest, this artist isn't as avante-garde as one might hope. I don't know that I see her work ever taking off in any grand sense, but I think they'll hold their value. And, really, they're so sweet and lovable that I carry them regardless of the low monetary value."

By her words Duncan, who knew nothing about art, expected the paintings to be twenty bucks or so. Instead they were a few hundred for the small ones, increasing in price after that. But he loved them, the first time he had ever felt a connection with a piece of artwork. He knew Birdie would love them but, more than that, he knew Darla would too, one day. Something about them reminded him of the farm, of visiting his grandparents and warm family gatherings. They were simple, with primary colors and homespun little scenes. All around them people were flocking to the modern pieces, splatters on canvas, neon blotches that looked like nothing. Duncan wouldn't have brought them home, even if they were free. But these...

"I'll take all of them," he declared with a nod, feeling good about the decision. Somehow he knew they were the perfect thing for his home. They were no doubt what Marlow had in mind when she began her design. So enamored was he with the sweet pictures that he brought her hand to his lips and kissed it. "You were right."

She leaned in, staring, eyes narrowed in concentration.

"What are you doing?" he asked, preemptively amused.

"Checking to see if your pupils are blown. Are you high?" she asked.

"I'm high on life," he said.

Avril laughed, delighted. She was trying to pretend her delight was in their repartee, but Duncan was a salesman. He knew it was more because of the three thousand dollars he'd just spent. He could probably punch her in the face right now, and she'd giggle delightedly.

She arranged to have the pictures shipped to his house, all but the smallest one she wrapped for him to take with him. He hugged it to his chest like precious treasure, and he felt like it was. Somehow these pictures embodied everything he felt about his home, his family, his world. Since Birdie left, he'd been fighting a losing battle with foreboding, as if nothing would ever be right again. But these pictures erased that. They opened everything back up, made the future seem not only possible but inevitable. The farm would be amazing; his life would turn out exactly as he'd planned, as he'd always imagined. Darla would be loved, happy, strong, would grow up with all the love and values Duncan had grown up with.

"I might burst into song," he warned Marlow as they left the gallery.

"I would love that," she said sincerely.

"You would," he said. His tone was derisive, but he reached his free arm around her and gave her a squeeze. "How you holding up?"

"I'm fine," she said easily.

He thought it was probably a blatant lie, but she seemed to need to keep the façade in place, so he let it slide.

"Marlow."

They froze because it was a voice they both recognized. "This city has a hundred and forty thousand people," Marlow muttered. And yet they ran into Jensen, the one person they were trying to avoid.

"We could just keep walking," Duncan said, arm now protectively tense on her shoulders. He wanted to turn and take a swing at the guy, but what right did he have? It would be utter hypocrisy for him to call another man out, especially for cheating, of all things. Faithfulness had never been foremost in his list of qualities.

"Might as well get it over with. I'll meet you back at the car, okay?" She stood on her toes and kissed his cheek. For appearances, for luck, for comfort, he didn't know and didn't care. He kissed hers in return and gave her shoulder an encouraging squeeze, purposely not looking at Jensen. He didn't know what he might do if he caught sight of the guy, and the thought was as enthralling as it was appalling. It would not do to have a street brawl in the middle of Savannah. On the other hand, it would be supremely satisfying.

Marlow took a breath. She forced her eyes to stop watching Duncan walk away. It felt like watching her parents drop her at the sitter and leave for work. *Don't go*, she wanted to call. On the other hand, she was a grownup who had business to attend to, namely in the form of her cheating boyfriend. So she took another breath and faced him.

"I didn't know you were still here," he said.

She didn't reply.

"Say something," he pled.

"Why didn't you just break up with me?" she asked.

"I didn't want to hurt you."

She blinked at him.

He sighed. "Yes, I hear it and know how stupid it sounds. I hurt you more by cheating."

"Did you ever love me?"

He flinched. "How can you ask me that?"

"Because when you love someone, you don't treat them this way, like garbage. Were you really going to be with her in the afternoon and me in the evening? Is there a morning girl, too? Do you have some kind of shift sign up?"

"No, it's not...it wasn't planned. She's a waitress at one of the clubs where I play, and she's been having a hard time lately."

"Well, I'm so glad you were able to kiss it and make it all better. Why are you telling me this?"

"Because I'm trying to explain."

"It really doesn't require an explanation. You cheated. The end."

He motioned impatiently toward her. "See, it's that."

"What?"

"So cut and dried, so together. Other girls would be falling apart, would be crying, but you, you're *fine*."

"I'm sorry, are you faulting me for having emotional maturity? Would you not have cheated on me if I cried more?"

"No, that's not..." He paused and let out a breath. "When we first got together, you were on drugs."

She flinched and pressed her lips together.

"I tried to be there for you as much as possible, to listen, to care. I felt like I helped you through that time, like you needed me." He paused, waiting for some acknowledgement. She nodded. "But since then... You don't need me. You don't need anyone. You left here, moved away without batting a lash."

"You never asked me to stay," she said.

"Why would I when you seemed so glad to go?"

"I swear I cannot win for losing." She pinched the bridge of her nose and took a shaky breath. "You met me when I was insecure, addicted to pills, and anorexic. I struggled out of that pit by the very tips of my fingers, earning sobriety, finally at long last becoming comfortable enough with myself and my body to eat a cheeseburger in public for the first time in five years. I did all the hard work it took to get to where I am today, secure, stable, sober, happy. And you're trying to tell me you liked me better then? Because it made you feel like more of a man to be needed?"

He shifted his weight and crossed his arms over his chest. "Of course that's not what I meant. I like you now, I *love* you. It's impossible not to, you're one of the best people I've ever known. It's just, I don't..." He looked away from her, guilty, and all of a sudden she got it.

She laughed, harsh and hollow. "You aren't attracted to me."

"Of course I am." He looked up and to the right, his tell that he was lying. "Maybe not as much as in the beginning. But that's not what this is about. We've had issues for a long time, and you know it."

Marlow didn't respond, simply turned and walked away. What was the point in staying? It wasn't as if they would get back together. He called to her; she pretended not to hear. Maybe Jensen believed their issues were deeper than her weight, and maybe that was true. But to Marlow, it was back to that, her one defining characteristic, the one thing everyone in the world seemed to cling to, no matter how hard she tried to let it go. The truth was that she was happy with herself as she was. Even, dare she say, liked the way she looked. She preferred herself curvy and healthy to stick thin and slowly dying. And wasn't that how it was supposed to be? Why did it seem like the world was upside down? Why did it feel like everyone else wanted her the reverse, to be thin at all costs, regardless of her physical and psychic misery? The unfairness bothered her more than anything else because it once again put the burden on her. In addition to finding peace with her size, which wasn't easy to begin with, she had to go the additional mile and find peace with the world's opinion on her body. And she had, mostly. But two of the people closest to her were the ones making it more difficult. Duncan didn't bother her as much because he was still in the baby pool of the adult world, new to feeling and thinking beyond himself. But Jensen…

She sucked a breath. Jensen hurt. She had no idea, none whatsoever that her weight was an issue for him. He had been with her as she became this size and for three years after that. Why hadn't he broken up with her? Was it because he loved her, or because he loved the version of himself that saw him as the type of guy who didn't care? He had aspirations of being deep, of being that guy who doesn't look at a woman's size. Was it possible it was a fear of disappointing himself that kept them together all these years? If so, how sad. How sad that she had loved him regardless, even when he'd been unemployed for ten months while recovering from a back injury. Even when he'd gone through the facial hair stage, regardless of the fact that his facial hair grew in patches, making him look like he suffered mange. Marlow hadn't cared about any of those things, had only ever cared about his heart. She'd thought his heart was good, but instead it was filled with loving himself, with idolizing the image of himself he'd created.

Duncan stood outside the car looking fretful. Not outwardly, not to anyone who didn't know him. To strangers passing by he looked cool, unaffected, ridiculously handsome and debonair against his expensive car. But Marlow saw the little furrow between his brows, the one that said he was worried. About her. Impossibly, she smiled and pelted herself at him, hugging him tight. He hugged her in return, resting his head on hers.

"Everything okay?" he muttered, his words muffled by her hair.

No, everything is awful. My faith in humanity is shaken, and I feel like I might never recover. "Of course," she said breezily. She let him go and faced the sun, shading her eyes and squinting to hide the sudden sting of tears. *Go away.* Not now, not ever. She was done crying over shallow, insincere boys. So many projects awaited her at home. Rather, Duncan's home. It would only be hers a while longer, and then what? *On to the next thing,* she thought, forcing a brightness she didn't feel.

It was a quiet ride back home. Duncan darted worried looks at Marlow, but she kept her face toward the window. He wanted to know what Jensen said. What excuse could he possibly come up with for hurting her that way? But he also didn't need to know because he had used them all before. So he let her bask in her quietness and solitude, not pressing the matter, another sign of his growth. He hated not knowing things, all the things. Hated being kept out of the loop in any way. But now, he realized, some things were too private and painful for him to be privy to. Marlow needed to keep her hurt private, for the sake of her pride. He'd let her have that; it was the least he could do.

When they arrived home, she changed clothes and began demolishing the kitchen.

"Need some help?" he asked. She seemed to be doing okay, but it would go faster if he did it with her.

"Sure," she said, tone pleasant and cheerful. He grabbed safety glasses and a sledgehammer and, together, they demolished the cabinets and counters.

"We should have rented the dumpster first," Marlow said, regretful.

Duncan privately agreed, but he wasn't in the mood to poke at her. "It's fine."

"I'll take care of it tomorrow," she said. She took off her safety glasses and set them on the dining room table. "I think I'm going to go to bed. I'm tired."

"All right," he said, watching her with a worried expression. There was nothing in her body language to suggest she was still upset, however. Her shoulders were in their rightful position, straight and proud. Her head was up, her breathing normal. He almost called to her, but decided instead to let her keep going.

With nothing else to do, he practiced guitar, but it felt stiff and forced without Marlow sitting nearby, judging him, urging him on. Eventually he turned in early, too.

Sometime in the night he woke to a sound. Since becoming a father, his ears had become attuned to every little sigh and whimper. He woke and stumbled to Darla's room before remembering Darla was still with her mother. Confused, he stood blinking outside her room, trying to orient himself enough to turn around and go back to bed, when he heard it again. A little whimper, a snuffle.

He inched forward to Marlow's door and leaned his ear to it. The sound was definitely coming from inside. His hand rose to knock, but he thought better of it. If he asked her, she would say she was fine. It was better not to give her the option. He opened her door.

She sat up, startled. "Duncan?"

"You're crying." He didn't mean for it to come out like an accusation, but it did.

"I'm fine." As if to convince him, or maybe because she simply couldn't sit up anymore, she lay down and curled into a ball.

He entered the room and lay down beside her. She held herself stiffly away from him, trying hard to repress her sniffles. "When Birdie went away, I cried myself to sleep for a week. It's the only time I've ever faked being sick and called off work."

Releasing her tears with a sigh, she rolled over and pressed her face to his chest, sliding her arm around him. He rolled to face her, gathering her close. "I hate this," she gasped.

"I don't," he said, almost but not quite happily. "I hate sleeping alone." He reached for the blanket and covered them both, snuggling her closer.

"More leg room that way," she noted, voice thick with tears.

"Leg room is overrated," he replied, putting his ankle over hers and drawing that part of her closer, too.

"Maybe," she agreed tentatively.

He kissed the top of her head and a minute later they were asleep.

CHAPTER 17

*I*n the morning, Duncan woke first. He and Marlow were mashed together in her too small bed, though he supposed it was possible they would have sought each other regardless of the bed's size, as they had in the hotel's king size one. He was tempted to linger, to wait for her to wake up and then... What? He had no idea. So he eased out of the bed and went to take a shower.

Later, when they met downstairs in the dining room, she didn't mention the night before, so neither did he. "I can't believe we demolished the kitchen," she said instead. "I think maybe that's my version of a tantrum."

"Your tantrums get a lot accomplished," he noted.

"At least I could have waited until it was Chelsea's portion of the week with Darla. I'll order the dumpster today and work on it tonight after she goes to bed."

"No rush," he said.

"There is, actually." She straightened and gave him a bright smile. "The day is almost here."

"What day?" he asked absently, his attention still on his phone and a work email he needed to answer.

"Gee, I don't know, maybe the day Birdie comes home," she said.

He jumped like he was jolted. "Oh, right."

"Don't tell me you forgot," she said.

"No, I guess I lost track of time a little," he said.

She reached over and gave his arm a squeeze. "Hey, are you okay?" Forgetting wasn't like him, especially not important things.

He nodded.

"Maybe you blocked it because you're feeling a little nervous. Too much pressure," she said, full concern now. "I feel bad. I've been pushing you too hard."

"No, hey, Marlow, no. You've done so much. It's crazy how much you've accomplished with this place, with me." He motioned to the house, accidentally encompassing the rubble of the kitchen.

She laughed. "It's possible I've been a bit too ambitious, but *you've* worked so hard. I want this for you so much. It's going to happen, I'm going to make it happen, even if I have to call in reinforcements." She bit her lip.

"What kind of reinforcements?"

"Tile. The truth is I don't know how to do it. I can learn, I *plan* to learn. But I'm afraid I won't be able to learn fast enough to do it well."

"I actually do know a tile guy, someone I went to high school with. I'll shoot him a text," he said.

"Excellent," she said, clapping her hands excitedly. "It's all coming together now. We should practice dancing tonight, too."

"You exhaust me," he noted absently, his attention back on his phone.

"Soon I'll be out of your hair forever," she promised. She returned to her cereal with renewed gusto. Duncan stared at the top of her head, his train of thought for work entirely gone.

It wasn't until later that morning at work that he finally remembered the file from her computer he had emailed to himself. He clicked on it, suddenly overcome with a giddy sort of curiosity. Marlow only ever told him what she wanted him to know. This was one thing he could discover for himself.

He clicked the file and sat back, blinking in surprise. A book, Marlow wrote a book. He started to read but the ringing of his phone reminded him he was at work. Somehow he made it to lunchtime and then sat at his desk, reading the entire hour.

He knew nothing about books, but he thought it was amazing. It kept his interest, and that was saying something. But maybe that was because he read it in Marlow's voice. Maybe he was so curious for a glimpse into her inner workings that he was biased. Before he could overthink it, he sent it to Sterling and asked him to read it and give his opinion, swearing him to secrecy.

DID YOU WRITE IT? Sterling responded.

HAHAHA. As if, he replied.

AFTER YOU ASKED to sing at my reception, I have no idea what to expect. You seem to be branching out.

IT'S ALL MARLOW, Duncan said.

I KNOW. That's why we like her, Sterling said.

ME TOO, Duncan thought, but he didn't say so because he had the idea Sterling and Alby hoped for romance between him and Marlow. Duncan hadn't said anything more about Birdie to Sterling because it was awkward, both because she was his sister and because he knew Sterling had started to approve of Birdie's boyfriend, Hayden Paxton. If Duncan were honest with himself, he was a little hurt by that. How could his best friend want anyone for Birdie but him? It should be the three of them, the way it had always been, the way it was always supposed to be. Plus Alby, of course. She made a pleasant addition to their trio. *And what about Marlow? Where does she fit?* He sat staring into space a long time, without ever coming to an answer.

By the time he arrived home, Marlow had half the kitchen demolition removed and loaded into the dumpster. "Naptime," she explained, holding her arms aloft in triumph.

"You should have been in the army. You get more done during naptime than most people do all day," Duncan noted.

"You know how it is," she said.

He did. He had been lucky enough to be able to take paternity leave. Those first few weeks, when it was just him and Darla, had been the most daunting of his life. He'd barely found the time to brush his teeth, let alone sleep or eat. It was better now, but not by much. "I should pay you more," he said for about the millionth time.

"But you won't," she finished the part of the sentence he usually finished himself.

"There are other perks," he said, tossing her an exaggerated wink. She wasn't there to see it, however. She was already outside, taking another load to the dumpster. "Is there a reason you're especially possessed with determination tonight?" Was she trying to avoid her feelings about the breakup?

"A guy at my dad's church does cabinets and counters. I begged and he's coming in two days to take measurements. He thinks he has something premade that will work, since the layout is simple."

"You're miraculous," he said sincerely.

"I do good puppy eyes," she said, batting her long lashes at him.

"I'd definitely install your cabinets," he said.

"How do you manage to make that sound naughty?" she asked.

"It's a gift." He spoke to her back as she left with another load of refuse. He'd been home ten minutes and she'd already cleared another quarter of the kitchen. If he waited long enough he might not have to do any of it. He took an exaggeratedly long sip of water.

"You need to call your friend," she said, breezing by him.

"Which one? I'm a popular guy," he said easily but had to wait until she came back for an answer.

"Tile guy."

"Ah, right. I'll shoot him a text right now." It was one more way to prolong the agony of carrying trash outside. He hadn't been exaggerating this morning; she really was wearing him out. He was ready to throw in the towel and admit he couldn't keep up with her.

"I'm onto you," she said, breezing by him again, arms loaded.

"What? I'm doing what you asked. I'm an innocent boy."

"I'm only allowing it because you're still in a suit."

"Suits buy me leeway?" he asked.

"Only when you make them look that good," she said, and now it was her turn to toss him the exaggerated wink.

Laughing, he sent a text to Reams, his high school friend. *Need a tile job, you up?*

At the farm? Reams texted back. All of Duncan's friends had spent time at the farm. His grandparents loved hosting parties, especially at Halloween though, if he were being honest, Duncan had only ever wanted Sterling and Birdie there for that. Somehow it had felt like their private holiday, family time.

Yes, redoing the kitchen.

Is tile picked out and purchased already?

"Marlow, have you bought the tile?"

"Yep, white subway. You'll love it."

He rolled his eyes, but didn't argue. By now he had learned to trust her judgment. *Already purchased, white subway.*

Grout, too?

. . .

"GROUT?" he called.

"Yep," she called back.

GROUT, *too. My nanny is crazy efficient.*

YOUR NANNY IS *in charge of your reno? Ten years out of school and your ability to make girls do stuff for you is nearing legend,* Reams replied.

HA, *meet her and you'll change your opinion. Marlow does what she wants.*

SOUNDS LIKE TRUE LOVE.

NAH, *we're good friends.*

DIDN'T THINK *you had girl friends.*

DUNCAN SCOWLED, not liking all the sentence left unsaid. Though, in Reams' defense, he only knew the old Duncan. This one was new and improved. *Have a daughter now. Have to be nice to girls.*

GOOD THING *I don't have a daughter,* Reams replied.

DUNCAN'S SCOWL INTENSIFIED. Reams wasn't a lady-killer, but he did all right. *Be nice to Marlow. Or else.*

. . .

*B*E NICE? *She a dog or something?*

H*E* COULDN'T ANSWER in any way that wouldn't arouse Reams' competitive side. *No, but good nannies are hard to find.* There, put the blame on Darla. Plus it was true, good nannies really were hard to find, especially ones that singlehandedly cleared a room of demo in, he checked his watch, twenty minutes.

I'LL BE NICE, Reams promised. Somehow Duncan was less than reassured.

CHAPTER 18

"You are a ruthless task master."

Duncan and Marlow once again lay on the floor, this time in his bedroom, too exhausted to move.

"But think about how much we've accomplished," she said, full throttle on enthusiasm.

He burrowed his head in her neck, nuzzling without admitting it was what he was doing. "You have a sickness."

Absently, she reached up to pet his head. Like a cat. "Let's recap. We have now successfully stripped the upstairs floors. And you said it couldn't be done." She nudged him.

"Can't talk, sleeping. And speaking of sleeping, where are we going to?" Along with the joy of learning how to use a floor sander for the first time, they'd also had to disassemble all the beds and Darla's crib, and then carry all the upstairs furniture downstairs.

"Obviously we'll have a campout in the living room," she said.

He perked up. Secretly he'd been hoping she'd cry again so he would have a reason to go in her room and comfort her. For a couple of nights he'd even hung around outside her door, holding his breath to listen. No such luck, though. She seemed completely mentally stable. More so than him, probably. "Will you tell me a story?"

So far he'd lacked the nerve to tell her he read her book, even though he enjoyed it. He was waiting to hear back from Sterling with a second opinion. What if he liked it because he liked her, but it was actually garbage? He wasn't a good judge of these things. Better to defer to the expert, a book-loving store owner. If Sterling hadn't been so good at football, he definitely would have been a geek. Maybe an über geek. In fact Duncan owed Sterling's nutjob dad a debt of gratitude. If he hadn't ignored every natural tendency in his sensitive, literary-minded son and pushed him hard toward sports, Sterling and Duncan might never have met.

"Now that we've rested…" Marlow began, and Duncan groaned.

"We haven't rested at all."

"We need to start on the varnish."

"No, I'm begging you," he said.

"You know we have to get it done before Darla comes home."

"Please make it stop. You're working me harder than my former football coach who made me run bleacher sprints for making out with his daughter."

She sat up to peer down at him. "You made out with the coach's daughter?"

Her hair had half slipped out of its bun. He twined it through his fingers, enjoying the silky feel. It was like the grownup version of a blankie. "In my defense, she was in college."

"Did you know it was your coach's daughter?"

He nodded, biting his lip.

"Duncan Shepherd, ladies and gentleman."

"Lie back, let me tell you more of my shenanigans." He held out his arm to her.

She used it to pull him up beside her. "You can talk while you varnish. You roll, I'll cut in at the edges."

"How can I talk when we have to wear a respirator?" he asked.

"You don't *have* to wear a respirator. Only if you don't want to sustain brain damage and, you know, for some of us it might be too late."

"If I weren't too exhausted to move right now, I would totally hunt you down and make you pay for that remark," he said.

"All we have to do is roll on this varnish and we can go downstairs and get all cozy. I will tuck you in and tell you a bedtime story and you can go to sleep. Doesn't that sound nice?" She stood on her toes and slipped the respirator over his head. He nodded yes, but he wasn't certain he meant it. The downstairs was a disaster area. Between all the furniture they'd trekked down and the mess from the kitchen, it was the very essence of a reno gone wrong. It stressed him to have things so torn up. Usually it would have made him cranky, but Marlow kept assuring him it was almost finished, that it always looked bad before it looked good.

They worked in silence. Once again Marlow was correct; the prep work and sanding were worse than the varnish. Basically it was like painting a wall, except the paint was a thin clear coat of varnish. The floors were original pine plank, not needing anything but a spruce. Marlow did all the requisite research about what to do and how to do it, meaning Duncan only had to show up and lend a hand.

They backed themselves to the stairs and stood on the top tread, admiring their handiwork. Marlow took off her respirator and set it aside, resting her head on him. "It looks so good," she whispered.

"So good," he agreed. He hugged her and rested his head on hers. She sniffed. "Are you crying or telling me I have BO?"

When she didn't answer, he looked at her face and saw that she was, indeed, teary. "Hey, what's wrong? Is it, you know, Jensen?"

She gave a watery little laugh and shook her head. "No. It's just so beautiful. It looks so amazing in here. I can envision how it's going to look when it's all put together, and I'm so happy for you." She returned his hug, squeezing hard.

A few times he had wondered what she was getting out of this, and he finally realized the answer was nothing. She was killing herself on his behalf, merely to try and make his dream come true, to see him happy.

"Let's have our campout," he whispered, giving her a squeeze.

"Sleepy boy," she said, patting his chest.

He was sleepy, his body exhausted. But it was more than that. He wanted to lie down and know she was beside him, if not in his arms then within touching distance. What he told her was true, he hated to sleep alone. He always had. He was that kid who sneaked into his parents' bed way too long, much longer than it was appropriate. He only stopped when he was in second grade and mentioned something to Sterling about it. Sterling had looked at him, horrified, and told him big kids like they were didn't sleep with their parents anymore. He had passed it off as if he were joking, but he wasn't. And he struggled through a few hard months of learning to sleep alone, something he accomplished but never grew accustomed to. Marlow was *right there.* And even though he didn't need Sterling to tell him it would be inappropriate to sneak into his roommate's bed each night, the temptation was strong. It was as if a switch had been flipped during her breakup so he found himself almost craving her presence, especially at night.

They took turns in the downstairs bathroom with Marlow going last. Duncan watched her with a sleepy expression as she exited the bathroom and began arranging her bed.

"Psst," he called.

She turned to face him.

He patted the spot beside him. She turned toward her bed, uncertain, and then back to his. He lifted the cover. "Your bed's not even made," he pointed out.

Sighing, she eased over and crawled into the blank space beside him. "You're going to get tired of always having me in your space," she said.

"Absolutely. You drive me crazy," he said, nuzzling his face against her neck again. She really did, though. She drove him crazy in all the ways, both good and bad.

"You're so perplexing. Mr. Cool and Independent who hates to be alone. I don't know quite what to do with you."

He meant to tell her he could provide some ideas, but he fell asleep before the joke could leave his lips.

The next day he came home to find Reams tiling his kitchen,

Marlow on standby like his apprentice, the two of them talking and laughing like old friends. Right away his jealousy went into overdrive. Marlow was his nanny, *his*. And since when did she do home reno with other people? That was their thing.

Then it was as if he could hear Marlow's warning voice in his head. *You don't own the people in your life; you can't treat them like possessions.* So he took a breath and forced a bright smile. "Hey. What y'all got cooking in here?"

"Nothing yet, but your new stove comes tomorrow," Marlow announced. She took his hands and he twirled her. Reams watched them with a smile that looked a bit too fond and possessive for Duncan's tastes.

"What's up, Shepherd?" Reams asked, tilting his chin in a nod.

"Nothin' much, Reams. It's looking good in here. What's new with you?"

"Nothin'. I'm just being *nice*." Smirking, he returned to his work. Reams was such a dog. Why on earth had he thought it would be a good idea to bring him on this job? The guy would probably hit on Darla when she came of age.

"Bad day?" Marlow asked, tone full of polite concern.

"No, why?"

"You're scowling something fierce."

Reams snickered.

"I'm warm, I guess," Duncan said, tugging his collar.

"It's a hot one out there today. Would you like a glass of tea?" She motioned to the refrigerator and he did a double take. Gone was his Grammy's old white monstrosity. In its place was a sleek new stainless steel number.

He whistled appreciatively as she handed him the tea.

"David, would you care for a glass?" she asked Reams. Duncan had almost forgotten his name, so long had it been since anyone called him anything but Reams. He and his best friend Stokes had been the replaceable everyman of their group, their features indistinguishable from each other, as well as every other kid in school, Sterling and Duncan notwithstanding. And Hayden Paxton had his own following back then, separate from theirs. He'd tended to attract all the artsy types. Smart and clever girls, girls like Birdie. Duncan eyed Marlow. Which way would she have gone, if she'd attended their school? Jock or artsy?

"What?" she mouthed, and he realized he was staring at her as he made his speculation.

"You're cute," he mouthed. She rolled her eyes, but she was smiling, cheeks slightly flushed. *Huh. Never seen that before.*

"Can you hand me that thing there, please, Marlow?" Reams asked with uncharacteristically charming manners. Duncan's brows snapped together. Had he been plying that tone on Marlow all afternoon? Was that the reason for her flush?

"You might need another sweet tea," Reams said, noting his thunderous expression with an amused nod.

"I'm maybe starting to get a headache," Duncan said.

"Oh, no, I bet it's the fumes," Marlow said, resting her hand on his shoulder. "My parents invited me to supper tonight. I'm bringing you along."

"Okay," he said in a pitiful tone. How far could he get with sympathy?

"Oh, shoot, I was going to ask if you want to get supper with me," Reams interjected.

"That's sweet, Reams, but I'm not interested," Duncan replied.

"Aren't you?" Reams said, shooting him a look.

Marlow was otherwise engaged, staring hard at a few pieces of tile she was attempting to arrange on the counter.

"I'll end you," Duncan mouthed to Reams, slitting his finger across his throat.

"I guess we'll always have tomorrow," Reams added.

"Hmm," Marlow said, emerging from her fog. "Darla comes back tomorrow. Oh," she faced Duncan, resting a hand on his arm. "Maybe we shouldn't go out tonight. Maybe we should stay here and work. Time is slipping away."

"Y'all on a deadline?" Reams asked.

"Yes, it's only two weeks until Birdie comes home," Marlow said, biting her lip worriedly as she stared at the general state of disrepair the house had become.

"What does Birdie have to do with the house?" Reams asked.

"We're using it as a general timeline," Duncan said smoothly. The last thing he needed was big mouthed Reams running to tell tales to the rest of their group from high school or, worse, Sterling. Something told Duncan he already had enough ammunition for a lifetime after this little interlude. "Birdie always loved this house. I wanted her to see it finished."

Marlow was now pressing her lips together, looking regretful. She probably thought all his friends knew his feelings for Birdie. How wrong she was. It had probably been Duncan's most closely guarded secret.

"You going to let Hayden tag along on that tour?" Reams asked, a skunky little smile on his stupid face. Why was he friends with this guy? At the moment, Duncan had no idea.

"Who is Hayden?" Marlow asked.

Duncan didn't answer, but of course the ever-helpful Reams did. "Hayden Paxton is Birdie's boyfriend."

"You know him?" Marlow asked.

"Know him? He was my neighbor down the street my whole life. We were friends when we were little, but then we switched groups. And of course no one who was friends with Sterling and Duncan could be friends with Hayden. Except Birdie, apparently." He grinned, the dope.

"You about finished?" Duncan asked.

"Nope," he replied happily.

"Huh," Marlow said, hands on hips.

"Hey, hadn't we better get to your parents? I know they eat early," Duncan said, his tone oozing respect and good breeding.

"If you think you can put me off by using my parents as a shield, you are sorely mistaken," Marlow said. Turning to Reams, she was once again all smiles. "Do you need anything before we leave, David?"

"I think I'm good, Marlow, thanks."

"You help yourself to anything from the fridge, you hear?"

Still smiling, Reams gave her a little nod. She turned and walked out the door, leaving heavy silence in her wake.

"Well, well, well," Reams said slowly, cheerfully. "Duncan Shepherd got a thing for the nanny. That is just too much." He laughed, shaking his head.

"You have no idea what you're talking about," Duncan said. "I told you Marlow and I are friends. I… there's someone else."

"There always is for you, isn't there? Well, that's good news for me, then. I suppose you won't mind if I ask her out tomorrow, for real?"

His tone was still light and teasing, but there was a hint of truth in it. He fully intended to ask Marlow on a date. "She's just out of a relationship, not ready to date yet."

"Then I reckon she'll tell me so when I ask her," Reams said.

"I already told you I don't want you to do anything to mess up her position here," Duncan said.

"Her position, hmm," Reams echoed.

Duncan pinched the bridge of his nose, borrowing a tool from Marlow's shed. "Let me try to say it in a language you'll understand. Ask Marlow on a date, and I will plant you so far into the ground they will never find the body."

"Ah, man, this is too good," Reams said, shaking his head, clearly amused.

"I'm trying to remember why we're friends," Duncan said.

"I've been trying to work that out the last twenty years," Reams replied easily.

Duncan pointed at him, looking stern and severe. "Lock the door when you leave, *David*."

In answer, Reams laughed, hard.

CHAPTER 19

Marlow stood leaning against the car, arms crossed as she waited for him.

"Did I mention you're cute?" he said.

"Nice try." He opened the door for her and she waited to speak until he was behind the wheel. "Why didn't you tell me Birdie's boyfriend was from here? Why did you let me believe she met some guy overseas?"

"Because I wanted it to be true."

Deflated by his sad tone, she reached out and rested her hand on his knee. "What's the real story?"

"He and Birdie became friends around the time she and I got together. And then..." he paused to look at her. He had no idea why he was hesitating. It wasn't as if she didn't already know what kind of man he was. "The thing is that I pursued Birdie on purpose after I found out about Chelsea, when we were still keeping it secret. I panicked, wanted our relationship to be set before the news broke. I pursued her hard until I thought I had her, and then I blurted the truth in the worst possible way. And she..." he broke off again, remembering Birdie's face in that moment, the pain, the way she'd flinched like he slapped her. *I hate you,* she'd yelled, and in that moment he knew she meant it. "She was hurt. I thought we could work through it because…" he took a breath and forced himself to say the next words. "Because it wasn't as if guys were lining up to get to her. She had never dated, not really. I felt confident we could work through our problems. But I didn't know she'd been talking to Paxton that whole time, becoming friends. When she went away to Italy, he followed. They've been together ever since."

She was silent, never a good sign.

Now that the words were tumbling out of him, he couldn't seem to stop them. "So, you see, it was my pride and arrogance that cost me what I love most. I was so certain of myself, of my place in Birdie's life and heart, that I wasn't careful with her heart, took it for granted. Assumed she would forgive me every indiscretion, would always be there waiting for me to get it together." He swallowed hard, feeling like the worst sort of idiot. These were all things he knew about himself, but he had never put them into words before, never looked at his behavior so starkly before. Somehow he always found a way to minimize it, but there was no minimizing it today. He had been a fool, and the only thing worse than a fool was an arrogant fool.

"Well, that complicates things a bit," she mused softly, giving his knee a comforting squeeze.

"Yeah, pretty hopeless, right?" He sighed.

"I don't know," she said slowly, and he perked up. "I'm not advocating we steal her away from this Hayden person. That lacks integrity. All I'm saying is that longevity counts for something, it counts for a lot. You and Birdie have history together, a long history. You've loved her for so long and you're doing so much work on her behalf. There is absolutely nothing wrong with presenting her with her options and hoping for the best." His expression must have still looked morose because she leaned closer and rested both hands on his leg. "Listen, I don't know this Hayden person, but I know you. You have worked so hard, come so far, Duncan. If I were Birdie and you presented me with what you're about to present, well." She shrugged.

He took her hand, twining their fingers together. "Are you trying to tell me you find me irresistible?"

"Not me, of course, but some women enjoy devastating good looks with the personality to back them up."

"But you're above that sort of thing," he said.

"That's right. I enjoy those diamonds in the rough. If a man is handsome, I don't want to be able to tell. It has to be buried under layers of imperfection. And if he has some good traits, I want to have to search for them. Ugly jerks, that's what I'm into."

"You're such a liar," he said, reaching out his free hand to brush her hair at her temple, soothed by its silky softness. "You'll fall in love with some pro footballer or something, some rich meathead who doesn't deserve you."

"I've given up on love."

"Don't say that. That's the recent breakup talking. You're going to be fine."

She shook her head, staring hard through the front window. "It's not worth it. I'm tired of being disappointed by people. If you don't try, you never get disappointed."

"Marlow," he began, but she forced a bright smile.

"We should get inside. My mom doesn't like to keep dinner waiting."

He reached for the door but hesitated. "Why are you parents okay with me?"

"They like you. No, they *adore* you," she said, rolling her eyes. Duncan's easy charm had worked well on her parents. If he were Baptist, they would probably try to make him a deacon.

"But why are your highly conservative parents okay with letting their precious baby daughter live with a man, much less a guy like me?"

"I'm twenty five. I make my own decisions," she hedged. He poked her. "They trust me, okay?" She couldn't, wouldn't tell him the humiliating truth. Even her parents didn't believe a guy like him would have anything to do with a girl like her. Her mother had said as much when Marlow first showed her his picture. *I bet his girlfriends are all size zero.* The joke was on them, she supposed, because he only wanted one girl, and she was probably closer to a four than a zero. But the sentiment was true. Duncan had made it abundantly clear he would never be interested in a fat girl. In the beginning, Marlow had laughed. She stared through the window now, wondering at what point it stopped being funny.

"Hey," Duncan said, reaching over to rub her earlobe between his two fingers, an oddly soothing motion. "You coming?"

She smiled, pushing away the unhappy thoughts. What was the point of having an insulating layer if not to use it to keep away all the feelings she didn't want to feel? "Absolutely. And when we get home, we're going to roll a second coat of varnish."

He groaned, staring hopefully at the house. "Maybe your parents can save me from your madness."

"Where do you think I get it? My dad once made us spend our entire spring break painting the house, and I was six."

"There's no escape," he said.

"Cheer up. If all goes according to plan, I'll soon be out of your hair forever."

They faced forward together, both frowning now for reasons neither was willing to contemplate.

CHAPTER 20

*B*irdie's arrival was a week away, and Marlow felt the pressure. She had promised Duncan a finished house, and she was trying hard to deliver. But she had a baby to watch every day, and time felt like it was slipping through her fingers. The big jobs were done and, if she let herself, she could be amazed by what they'd accomplished in a relatively short amount of time. In four months they had painted every ceiling in the house, refinished the floors, both up and downstairs, painted all the walls, torn out and re-done the kitchen, and renovated the bathroom in Duncan's room. Now that it was down to the details, it should be easy. All Marlow had to do was change out some light fixtures, clean, hang the paintings, and arrange all the furniture and accessories. Plus the secret projects she'd been working on for the dining room. *It's kind of a lot,* she admitted. Not for the first time, she had backed herself into a corner, bitten off more than she could chew. But she was a goal-oriented person. Go big or go home, that was her life motto.

"I can do this," she said out loud, trying hard to believe it.

Duncan noted her busyness with disapproval. "You are killing yourself. You have to slow down."

"I'm so close to being done," she said, checking her list for the eighth time in the last hour, hoping something had miraculously been checked off since the last time she looked.

Duncan snatched the list from her fingers and set it aside. "Let's take a break and do something fun."

"I don't have time for fun."

He placed his hands on her shoulders and shook her. "Do you even hear yourself right now?"

For a moment she looked torn between laughter and tears, and then laughter won. She sputtered. "Yes, I'm insane."

"You really are." Now his fingers were rubbing soothing little circles on her shoulders. "And while I appreciate that your insanity gets a lot accomplished, you're way too frazzled. So I'm busting you out. Let's go have fun."

"Doing what?"

He froze. "I hadn't gotten that far."

She gathered his shirt in her hands, thinking fast. "I could really stand to blow off some steam. I need to decompress."

"What," he paused to clear his throat, "what did you have in mind?"

She gazed up at him, big eyes dewy, full lips slightly parted. "One on one."

He blinked at her. "What?"

"Let's shoot some hoops."

"You play basketball?"

She tipped her head, annoyed by his incredulity.

"Of course you play basketball. You can do all the things. Where should we play, LeBron? It's a million degrees outside."

"My dad's church," she said with sudden enthusiasm. "The fellowship hall has a basketball court."

"Okay," he said, catching her enthusiasm. He hadn't played ball in forever. He and Sterling usually tried to play a few times a month, but they had both been busy lately with their various projects, he with the house and baby and Sterling with his upcoming wedding and bookstore. When had they turned into such genuine grownups?

"You went pensive," she noted.

"It's been a long time since I played," he said.

"Me too. I'm probably a little rusty," she said.

"I promise to take it easy on you," he said, hooking his arm around her neck.

"Same," she said, giving his waist a squeeze.

He thought she was joking. He should have known better. He was a better player, but she played dirty, and she played hard. And today she was out for blood.

"That has to be a foul," he said from his position on the floor where she'd knocked him when she blocked his shot and stole the ball.

"Cry more," she said, sinking the shot.

In the end she won by two points, but unlike usual, Duncan didn't care because he had so much fun. "You are a dirty little cheater," he said, picking her up and spinning her in a circle.

"Creative use of the word little," she said, laughing as she whirled.

"You're littler than me," he said, strangely elated over the knowledge that he could pick her up. He hadn't tried before, for fear he wouldn't be able to and then they would both feel awkward, but he was holding her fine, didn't even feel strained or winded.

"Give it time," she said, and he laughed.

"Nah, I think you've lost weight." He set her down and scanned her as if trying to judge whether or not she'd shrunk. In reality he was merely appreciating the sight of her rosy cheeked and covered in sweat. He swallowed hard and reached for the water he'd brought, throat suddenly dry.

She reached for her water. Was she eyeing him with the same amount of appreciation, or was it his imagination?

"Like what you see?" he asked.

"Sweat works for you," she said, tipping her water toward him like a little toast.

"More where that came from," he said, wagging his brows.

"Excellent." She took a step closer and rested her palm on his chest. "Let's go home and you can," she stood on her toes to whisper in his ear, "rearrange the furniture."

He laughed. "Your powers of seduction leave a lot to be desired."

"I'll keep working on them," she promised.

"See that you do," he said, taking another swig of water. They'd been joking, but now there was a sudden tense awareness between them and neither of them knew what to do next. So when one of their phones buzzed, they both lunged for them, nearly clunking heads in their haste to break the moment.

"Mine," Duncan said, snatching it up with a frown. "It's Chelsea."

Marlow tensed. To her knowledge, Chelsea had never contacted Duncan before. Her tension grew as she watched his face drain of color. He said okay twice and the call ended.

"What?" she whispered, clutching his free hand.

He gripped her hand fiercely and whispered, "There's been an accident."

CHAPTER 21

Duncan let Marlow drive his Audi to the hospital, a sign of his extreme upset. "I'm going to take full custody," he declared after twenty minutes of silence.

"Duncan," she said, tone full of warning.

"What? She's completely irresponsible, totally unfit to be a mother. Darla is better off with me."

"Duncan," she said again, gently this time. "I know you're afraid and worried right now. But don't see Chelsea like this, please. You guys have been doing so well co-parenting. But if you go in like this, you're going to do irreversible damage. And what you said is not true. Chelsea is a good mother. I see her almost every single day and Darla is always clean, well fed, content. It's as hard for Chelsea to say goodbye each day as it is for you. She's a good mom, and she adores Darla."

He scowled at her. "You're supposed to be on my side."

"No, I'm supposed to be on the side of truth and reason," she said, but kindly. "Hey, it's going to be okay. Tell me what Chelsea said again."

He squeezed his eyes closed. "She said she and Darla were in an accident but Darla's seat held up well. She wasn't even crying or upset when they took her to the hospital." He faced her, eyes blazing, "But how could she let that happen? And how could she possibly be separated from Darla? She's a tiny little baby. She can't go to the hospital on her own."

"We're almost there," she said soothingly, knowing nothing else would work. "Just please, please don't barge into the hospital and steamroll Chelsea. Reserve judgment until you hear what actually happened, okay? Please."

"If she was drunk, I..." he trailed ominously away, turning to stare out the window, hands clenched.

She reached across the console and took his hand, prying it open to give it a squeeze. He gripped it painfully like a lifeline the remaining way to the hospital. Chelsea was still in the emergency room when they arrived. Duncan charged ahead, leading Marlow behind him like a little tugboat. He yanked open the door to Chelsea's room and stopped short. She was in a neck brace, immobilized from the chest down by splints on her arms, face bruised and swollen, lips split and bleeding.

"Oh, honey," Marlow said, letting go of Duncan to rush forward and press her hand to Chelsea's forehead, the only part of her that looked remotely touchable.

Chelsea burst into tears, gasping in pain. "They won't let me see her, I can't get any information." She tried to turn her head toward Duncan but couldn't. "You have to go be with her. I don't even know where she is."

"We'll find her," Marlow promised when Duncan remained mute. "What happened?"

"A guy ran a red light and t-boned me. They think he was drunk. If Darla's car seat hadn't been on the opposite side of the car." She tried to shudder and her tears came faster, turning into hiccupping sobs.

"Hey," Marlow soothed. "Shh, Chelsea, it's okay. That didn't happen. Darla's going to be fine. We're here, everything is okay."

Chelsea's eyes opened and fastened on Duncan. "Please don't take her away from me. It wasn't my fault."

He flinched, either at the raw pain in her voice or her accurate assumption that he would try. "No, hey." He reached out a hand but had no idea where to put it, so it hovered tentatively above her, like he was about to bestow a blessing. Maybe he was. "Chelsea, no. You're her mom. A girl needs her mom, and you're a good one. We're in this together, okay?" Across the bed, Marlow reached for a tissue and gently wiped Chelsea's cheeks, then returned to smoothing the hair off her forehead, soothing her. Chelsea let out a little sigh and seemed to sag.

"Will you go to her, please? I'm so worried about her."

"Yes, of course, and we'll update you. Can we call someone to come be with you?" Marlow asked.

"My stepdad is on his way," she said.

"I didn't know you had a stepdad," Duncan commented. It was first on the list of things he didn't know about her, namely because he had never cared to take the time to ask or learn. He was having another one of those insights into his poor character. Chelsea was his child's mom. They would be connected until Darla was at least eighteen, and maybe even after that. He should at least know the basic facts of her life.

Chelsea attempted to smile but couldn't. "Sometimes stepparents turn out to be amazing, good news for us, huh?"

He smiled and it felt like peace he didn't realize he needed. He and Chelsea didn't have to be in love, they didn't even have to be friends. But they were family in a manner of speaking. Finding a middle ground between loathing and romance would be a nice change for all of them.

"We'll call your dad with updates, I have his number," Marlow assured her.

"They think both my arms are broken. Darla's going to have to stay with you a while," Chelsea said, her tears beginning again.

"Of course," Duncan said, trying not to feel elated. He *was* sorry to see Chelsea in such poor shape, but he wasn't sad for the extra time with his daughter.

"I'm going to miss her so much," Chelsea sniffed.

"I'll bring her over to visit all the time, I promise," Marlow said. "She's going to miss you, too, you know. We'll be over so much you'll probably tell us to go away."

"We're so lucky Duncan found you. I don't know what we'd do without you," Chelsea said.

"Same," Duncan agreed.

"Quit that," Marlow said, cheeks flushed. She gave Chelsea's head another pass. "I'll call soon with an update, okay? And have your dad call us if you need anything."

"Okay, thank you," Chelsea said, sniffling.

Duncan took Marlow's hand and led her back out of the emergency room to registration, where they were informed Darla had been re-routed to Children's Hospital across town. Marlow laid a restraining hand on Duncan who looked ready to explode at the news that his child had been moved without his consent.

"Her mother consented," the lady at registration informed them.

"She probably had no idea what she was consenting to," Marlow said. Chelsea hadn't exactly been in the best shape.

"I know, it's just…I just want to get there and see for myself she's okay."

"I know. Want me to drive again?"

"I'm good now, thanks," he said, though he gripped the wheel until his hands turned white, remaining tense and silent the whole drive. Marlow didn't know what he might do if they weren't allowed to see Darla right away, but they were ushered to her room immediately.

Darla lay in the center of the room, asleep in a crib that looked like a metal cage. She wasn't hooked to any tubes or monitors, but she was completely out, not stirring when Duncan rested a hand lightly on her chest. It was as if he needed to reassure himself of her even, steady breathing. They stood on opposite sides of the crib, staring at her in silence until the doctor arrived to update them on her condition.

"During transport, she seemed to experience some discomfort. I suspected she might have a fracture, so we did an x-ray and gave her a light sedative. It was not a general anesthetic, but it had the effect of making her sleepy. She'll be out for a few hours. The x-ray noted a slight fracture of her collarbone."

"Is that serious?" Duncan asked, gripping Marlow's hand.

"I assure you it's not," the doctor said. He had a pleasant, calming Indian accent. Marlow had the strange thought that she would love to hear him narrate an audiobook. "To set it in a cast would be more disruptive to her at this point. It should heal nicely on its own, but you'll need to take care in how you lift her. No yanking from under her armpits, cradle her, scooping her whole body at once as you pick her up. Over the counter pain meds will work well, if you feel she's having discomfort. Otherwise she'll be fine. We'll keep her overnight for observation, until the effects of the anesthesia wear off. You are both welcome to stay with her."

They shook hands and the doctor departed. After staring at Darla a while longer to reassure themselves she was really okay, Duncan sank into the uncomfortable recliner, pulling Marlow into his lap. He pressed his face to her neck, gripping her tightly as he released a shaky breath.

"Let's never do this again, okay?" he said, aiming for levity and failing when his voice quavered. Marlow didn't answer. He glanced up and saw tears streaming down her cheeks. "Hey, what gives?"

"I was so afraid," she said, reaching for a tissue to press to her face.

"But you were so brave and calm," he said.

"Obviously I was faking, Duncan. Only one of us can fall apart at a time, that's the rule. Your turn is over, so gimme." She released a little sob and pressed the tissue harder to her face.

He peeled her hand away. "Why do you always hide when you cry? I like it when you cry."

"Weird," she whispered, sniffling, but her emotional burst seemed to be waning. "Why?"

"Because I like to comfort you." His hand eased to her face, tipping it toward his so he could see her better. Her perfect lips were puffy and red, aqua eyes dewy with unshed tears. "So gorgeous," he breathed, and then he kissed her. Or maybe she kissed him. Later neither would be able to remember who initiated the kiss, who reached desperately for whom, only that one moment they were staring at each other and the next they were a tangle of lips and limbs, trying in vain to melt into each other, hands in hair, mingled breaths coming in shallow gasps like dying fish. They had found a pause where neither of them thought about anything. Instead they acted on instinct, not realizing their instinct had somehow become dependent on each other for everything. The moments went on and on until Marlow sat back with a gasp, in a sudden shock of surprise.

"What are we doing?"

"Don't care, don't stop," Duncan murmured, yanking her closer again by the hem of her shirt.

"Kay," Marlow replied, lips landing on his again with an echoing and possessive need. Behind them Darla gave a shuddery little snuffle and they froze, lips together, some semblance of sense returning. Marlow leaned back, putting space between them, cheeks flushing as they dropped their hands in sudden and combined embarrassment. "We're both under duress. Lots of emotion."

Duncan nodded his agreement and took a shaky breath. "It's no big deal. Crazy things happen after a big event like this. All the time. I've heard stories. Lots…lots of stories. Of people. Duress."

"It won't be weird now between us, will it?" she asked, biting her swollen lip.

With effort, he resisted the urge to tug it free and kiss her again, clutching his hands into painful claws and swallowing hard as he stared longingly at her lips. "Nope."

"Good. I should go call Chelsea's dad and give him an update."

One of his hands worked free and tucked a silky strand behind her ear. "Better leave this part out."

She rolled her eyes, but she was smiling, the embarrassed flush beginning to fade. She stood and he swatted her on the behind. "It slipped," he said, pointing to his hand as if it were the outlying offender.

"You're such a guy," she said.

"Clearly," he said. "By the way, I think that brought our chemistry up to a six, maybe a seven."

"Ignoring you now," she said, reaching for the door.

He waited until she was definitively gone before he sneaked to the bed and leaned close to whisper in Darla's ear. "It was a solid eleven."

CHAPTER 22

The next week when Duncan arrived home, the most amazing smell greeted him at the door, along with Marlow who stood in the entry, blocking it with her body.

"What's up?" he asked.

"My parents were here today," she said.

"Okay. Are they holding you hostage and that's why you're acting so creepy?" She had her hands up, blocking his view of the inside.

"No, my dad helped me do some house stuff while my mom watched Darla and cooked supper."

"That's so nice," he said. He loved her parents, had come to think of them almost like family. Like Marlow, they were always willing to drop whatever and help out.

"The thing is, I'm done."

He blinked at her, mind fuzzy with sudden panic. Surely she wasn't quitting on him. The atmosphere had been a tiny bit weird since the kiss, with both of them pretending nothing ever happened, but nothing had seemed so drastic. He gripped the doorframe. "What?"

"I finished the house," she said softly, clasping her hands together beneath her chin in excitement. "Close your eyes."

He obeyed. She took his hand and led him into the middle of the living room. "Open."

He opened his eyes, and his mouth, as he stared around the room in amazement. It was as if she reached into his head and drew out the dream of exactly what the farm should look like. "Marlow," he breathed. The green velvet couch arrived a few weeks ago, but they'd left it covered in plastic because of all the construction dust. Now it was front and center in the room, Marlow's chunky afghan artfully draped on one edge. The room was a riot of color and texture, cozily tied together with all the homey little touches she'd placed there. "It's perfect, it's so perfect."

"C'mere," she said. Taking his hand, she led him into the dining room. As a kid, it had always been the heart of the home with family gatherings, friends, food, fun.

"Wha…wha…" he stuttered, actually stuttered for the first time in his life. His grandparents' old farm table, the one they'd moved to the basement when the reno began, was once again in its rightful place, only it had been fully refinished.

"I've been working on it in the basement, hence all the fumes. Sorry about that."

"You…you…" it seemed words were beyond him now. His glance fell to the floor and a massive braided rug. He pointed. "Where?"

"I made it," she said, sounding uncharacteristically shy.

He faced her, his rapid blinks transmitting the fact that his brain short circuited the minute he walked in the house. "You made it?" he drawled, uncomprehending. People didn't make rugs, did they?

"It's not so hard," she said, shrugging, embarrassed. "You sew a bunch of strips of material together and braid them."

"That's why you were sewing all those things?" he said. His eyebrows must be touching his hair by now.

She nodded and poked him. "Bet you feel pretty bad for making fun of me now, huh?"

He had teased her relentlessly, comparing her to the Amish, to the pioneers. He thought she was doing some girly craft. It never once occurred to him she was making something for him, on top of all the other work she was already doing on his behalf. "Marlow," he said, half accusing now.

She jumped. "What?"

He spun in a helpless little circle, taking in the unmitigated perfection of his dining room. The floors looked like new, the ceiling was bright and clean, the walls a soothing shade of white, the perfect artwork perfectly hung and arranged, his grandparents' table newly refinished, the crystal chandelier centered over it, a rug she'd hand-made for him the ultimate accompaniment. "This is so…it's just…why would you do this for me?" He sucked a deep breath and pressed his hand to his eyes, trying hard not to unman himself and cry.

She reached out a hand and laid it gently on his forearm. "Because it was what you wanted."

He scrubbed his sleeve over his eyes. "But I get all of this out of it, for the rest of my life." He motioned helplessly to the room again. "What's in it for you?"

"Your happiness," she said softly, as if it should be obvious. And she meant it, he knew. She had practically killed herself for months on end merely because she wanted to help make his dream come true. The disparity between them had never felt greater. She was so selfless; he was so…not.

"I can never repay you for this," he said.

She laughed, shrugging. "Why would you need to?"

He remained staring at her, speechless, not knowing how to begin to thank her. *Kiss her,* his brain screamed at him. It had started doing that at odd intervals now, ever since they brought Darla home from the hospital. He had ignored it, but today he wasn't certain he wanted to.

Marlow spun away, likely reading his face correctly. She had been careful not to get too close to him, always keeping Darla or one of her projects between them. "We should eat while it's still hot. My mom tried a new recipe for pot roast and I sneaked a bite. It's by far the best thing she's ever made."

"I don't think so," Duncan said, reaching out to give the back of her neck a squeeze.

She shrugged away from him on the pretense of pulling the roast out of the oven, but her too-pink cheeks told him she was embarrassed. She was fine with being told she was beautiful, but compliments about her character seemed to overwhelm her. In a good way, he hoped. "You hush," she commanded.

Duncan reached for an avocado and sliced it for Darla who had finally started eating solids. With gusto.

"She's going to need another bath," Marlow noted as Darla picked up an avocado slice and mashed it into her face.

"I'll do it," Duncan said, smiling as he watched the baby devour her food.

"You're such a good dad, Duncan," Marlow said. She arranged his plate of food and set it before him, waiting to speak again until she made one for herself and sat down. "Are you ready for tomorrow?"

"What's tomorrow?" His mind blanked. He was too busy staring at her, thinking she was a good surrogate mom, a good everything.

Marlow gave him a look. "Are you joking with me? What's tomorrow?" She motioned around the house. "What's all this been leading up to? It's the day Birdie comes home."

He jumped to attention, giving his head a little shake. "Right, I got caught up thinking about the house, sort of pushed everything else aside."

"Even Birdie?" she said, eyebrows aloft in incredulity.

"It's a really great reno," he said, smiling.

"I wish I could be there to judge her reaction when she gets off the plane," Marlow said, tone wistful. Duncan was going with her family to greet her at the airport tomorrow.

"Come with me," he said, realizing it was an amazing idea. He wanted Marlow there, needed her. For moral support, of course.

"I can't intrude on family time," she said, frowning.

"You're my family, you dolt. Plus Darla does better when you're holding her lately." He glanced at Darla as if assuring himself she was still okay. He had been doing it since they brought her home from the hospital, an anxious habit. She seemed fine, but occasionally she had an obvious twinge of pain that made her howl. Marlow seemed to know how to hold her correctly to ease the ache of her poor little broken collarbone.

"She likes my softness," Marlow said, also staring concernedly at Darla.

"She's not alone in that," Duncan blurted and pressed his lips together.

Marlow laughed, probably believing he was joking. He wasn't. Lately he felt like he needed to sit on his hands to stop them reaching for her. She was so pleasant and comforting to hold. It eased something inside him, some ache he didn't know existed. He glanced at his baby daughter again, not certain he wanted to have this thing in common with her.

"I really want you to come with me to the airport tomorrow. Please? Birdie is dying to meet you."

"All right, but only because I'm nosy and intrusive, not because this charm offensive in any way works on me."

"Incentive to try harder then," he said.

"Please don't," she said, and he couldn't tell if she was joking.

CHAPTER 23

They were both nervous on the way to the airport. "I know why I'm nervous. Why are you nervous?" Duncan asked, darting Marlow a look. Or maybe two or three. She had gone all out on her appearance again, for the first time since her breakup with Jensen. At this rate they'd be lucky if he didn't drive them into a ditch. He forced his head forward, gripping the wheel to try and keep it there.

"What if she doesn't like me? Or what if I don't like her? I've heard about her for so long that I've kind of built her up in my head as this paragon of perfection," Marlow said.

"She's not like that," Duncan said. "She's sweet and fun, the quintessential little sister. You'll see. You already like Sterling, right?"

"Yes."

"Well, there you go."

"But just because I do well with the brother doesn't mean I will with the sister. They're not conjoined."

"Be weird if they were," he said.

"You're trying to cajole me out of my nerves," she accused.

"I'm trying to cajole both of us. I haven't seen her in a year, and when she left…things weren't exactly easy between us. I, uh, maybe said some things I shouldn't have when she went away." He had accused her of being selfish, of being a coward, of running away to avoid her feelings for him.

"That was the old Duncan. Today she'll meet the new one," Marlow said confidently, giving his leg a little pat. He caught her hand and held it in a comforting clasp. He was probably squeezing a little too hard, but she didn't call him on it.

Duncan wanted to carry Darla, mostly to give his hands something to do, but she preferred Marlow now in all things. "She likes you better now," he pouted.

"Don't be ridiculous. You're her *Daddy*. Absolutely no one on earth can take your place."

"I know," he said. They paused and faced each other. He reached out and rubbed her earlobe. She reached up and did the same. He smiled. "What are you doing?"

"You always do this to me, and it's so soothing. I thought I would help you relax, too."

"I don't do it to relax you. I do it because I like your ears. They're adorable."

"All this time and I never knew you were an ear guy. So weird, Duncan. So, so weird."

"I don't like everyone's ears. Just Marlow."

"Sweet, but no less weird."

"Hush, you," he said.

"Why are you rubbing each other's ears? Are you thinking of getting a dog?" Sterling and Alby came up on their right, along with Sterling's mom.

"Where's your dad?" Duncan asked.

"Don't ask," his mom said. Her tone told him it was a sore subject, so he dropped it immediately. Instead he turned his focus to Alby, whistling appreciatively. "Looking sharp, Ms. Mowry."

"Thank you, Duncan," Alby said, smoothing an imaginary wrinkle from her dress. "Do I look okay, really? Not too much?" she whispered in an aside to Marlow.

"Alby, you look amazing."

"I'm so nervous," Alby blurted. "Sterling thinks I'm crazy because I've known Birdie forever and she's a total sweetheart, but I've never met her as Sterling's, you know, *intended*. It's a lot of pressure."

"She is going to adore you," Marlow said with confidence. It would be impossible not to adore Alby, one of the kindest people Marlow had ever met. "And if not, who cares? You've got yours, sugar." She nodded toward Sterling who, even involved in conversation with Duncan and his mom, still kept half his attention on Alby.

Alby snorted a laugh and pressed her hand to her mouth. "Marlow, you're so funny. I'm so glad you're here." Her tone turned pensive again as her gaze swung toward the gate. Everyone turned to watch as passengers began to disembark. Marlow wondered if she would recognize Birdie on sight, having only seen her in the picture on Duncan's nightstand. But she had no trouble, mostly because her hair looked like it had grown to four times its normal size during the course of the flight. She had tried to contain it in a clasp, but it kept springing free, forcing her to push absently at it, annoyed. That was when Marlow took stock of the man beside her who also added a hand in trying to contain her hair.

"What do they feed the men in your town?" she whispered to Alby at her first sight of Hayden Paxton.

"He's not that nice looking," Duncan said, peeved.

He was, though. Feature to feature, Duncan was better looking. Sterling, too. But Hayden Paxton had that *thing*, that special cerebral quality that signaled to women he was wounded in some way only they could heal. It wasn't that he was sad, but he was so self-contained, so in his head that it made you want to take a peek inside his brain and see what was going on. If Marlow were honest with herself, he was exactly her usual type and she had to quickly tamp down any initial attraction on her part, reminding herself he was Birdie's. And Duncan's nemesis. That alone made him off limits. She was team Duncan, all the way.

"Might want to wipe the drool off your chin," Duncan said, scowling at her.

"What are you looking at me for, stupid? She's over there," she hissed, nodding her head in Birdie's direction.

His mouth quirked and he kissed the tip of her nose before facing forward.

Men, Marlow thought. There was something seriously wrong with them, Duncan especially. He had spent months extolling Birdie's virtues, waiting with baited breath for her to come home. And then when it was finally his moment, he wasted time being possessive over Marlow's attention. What would it matter to him if she *were* attracted to Hayden Paxton? Not that she would be, but still. She'd be doing Duncan a favor by taking him off Birdie's hands, if one were to look at things logically.

Sterling was the first to reach Birdie, picking her up in a bear hug and spinning her in a circle while she squealed and hugged him in return. Hayden stood by, smiling serenely, as if it made him happy to see Birdie happy. He had no family to greet him at the airport, and that was very sad. Marlow wanted to ask Duncan what happened to his family, but now wasn't the time because it was almost his turn to greet Birdie. It would have been gawking to watch, so instead she watched Hayden watch Birdie and Duncan hug and exchange a heartfelt greeting, "Hi, Duncan," from her and, "It's so good to see you," from him. Either Hayden had a good poker face or he was supremely secure because his smile only looked pinched for a second during the hug.

And then suddenly Birdie was in front of Marlow, her full focus on the baby. "Oh, my goodness," she said and started to cry gently. "Duncan she's just...she's even more beautiful in person." Her eyes flicked to Marlow. "Both of them. Hi, Marlow, I'm Birdie."

"It's so great to finally meet you," Marlow said sincerely.

"Same," Birdie said, but her attention was anxious to return to Darla who put on a good show, kicking and squirming with glee. "I know she's a little injured, but would it be okay if I held her? I've been dying to for nine long months now." Strangely she seemed to be asking Marlow's permission.

"Of course," Marlow said, extending her arms. Darla went eagerly to Birdie, lunging for her hair, trying to stuff all of it in her mouth. Duncan laughed and untangled it, much to Darla's annoyance. She screamed when he peeled the wad of hair from her greedy grasp.

"She has leadership skills," Duncan explained over her wailing.

"Like her dad," Birdie said, and that was when Marlow was certain they'd be friends. Birdie and Duncan walked together, she enraptured with the baby, he darting her looks as if trying to convince himself it was all real.

"Miss Marlow, I've been dying to meet you," Hayden Paxton said, coming up on her right.

"If you're looking to form an alliance because we're both outsiders, I should tell you I'm already in one with Duncan," she warned him.

He threw his head back and laughed, earning curious glances from the rest of their group, minus Duncan who tossed him a scowl. "I knew from Sterling and Alby's description I was going to like you," Hayden said.

"What did they say?" Marlow asked.

"Sorry, I can only tell secrets to people I'm in an alliance with," he said, and now it was her turn to laugh.

"Oh, my lands, we're going to get along just fine, Hayden Paxton," she said.

"You don't have to use both my names," he said.

"But now that I've started, I don't think I can stop, Hayden Paxton." He laughed again. "Girl, you're good entertainment."

"That's why Duncan pays me the big bucks. For my floor show." She gave him jazz hands, and he laughed again.

"Hayden," Duncan said, interrupting them with an outstretched hand. "It's nice to see you again. I'm glad you had a safe trip."

Hayden stopped short and took the proffered hand. It was either that or fall over Duncan's inert form. "Duncan, thank you. You're looking well. Fatherhood agrees with you, congratulations. She's adorable."

"Thank you." Duncan smiled, but remained frozen, blocking their path, forcing Hayden to move away.

"I guess I'll catch up with Birdie," he choked, covering his mouth with his hand and coughing a couple of times.

"What was that about?" Marlow asked.

"I don't know. Guy's always been weird," Duncan said.

"Not him, you."

"Me? What did I do? Did you see how nice I was to him? I shook his hand, Marlow. Now I have to burn it. And people call me a flirt." He glared hard at the back of Hayden's head.

"What are you talking about?" she asked.

"Nothing. He better stay away, is all."

"From his girlfriend? That seems like a lot to ask at this juncture," she said. They had paused to talk, but the rest of the group kept going.

"We're losing them."

"We should. It's too much, too soon. I need time to process. Let's just go home," Duncan said, massaging his temples.

"Um, crazypants, your daughter is with them. I can see now why you brought the nanny along, to remind you you're a father."

He grinned at her. "Yes, Marlow, that is undoubtedly why I brought you along." He turned his back to her. "Hop on."

"Hop on what?"

"The tram. A unicycle. One foot. Or my back, woman. And you call me crazy. What is this the universal sign for?" He pointed to his crouched position.

"In our case it's apparently, 'Please snap my spine.' There is no way you can carry me on your back."

"Of course there is. I'll prove it. Hop on."

"No way. It's undignified."

"This from the woman who jabbed me in the kidney when I went up for a layup," he said.

"That was an accident. I was aiming for your spleen," she said.

He bent over laughing and pointed to his back again. "Get on."

"No way."

"Do it, or I'll carry you front ways. Like Darla. People will stare. They might call security."

"Oh, my lands, Duncan. You have flipped your lid," she said, climbing on his back, cheeks flaming. She was certain she would be too heavy, would fall right off.

Duncan straightened and started to walk. "See? Easy peasy."

"You know we put that phrase on the list of things," she said.

"I think that list needs a lot of reworking," he mused.

"I don't understand one single thing that's happened in the last three hours," she said. "Why are you here with me instead of with Birdie, the person we came to see?"

"I'm giving her a chance to…bond with Darla. And…talk with Alby."

"Why are you talking like William Shatner?"

He snorted a laugh and stumbled.

"Oh sweet mercy, I've snapped your spine. We're going to go down like a demolished building," she said, gripping his neck tighter.

Laughing, trying hard to get a breath, he finally managed to say, "Marlow, I swear," just as they reached their group. Birdie swiveled to look at him. They locked eyes and he remembered all the many, many times he'd said the same thing to her, exasperated beyond measure. *Birdie, I swear.* She smiled at him, likely thinking the same thing he was. He smiled in return, tossing her a little wink.

CHAPTER 24

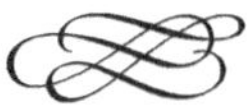

A *pool party. Kill me now.* Marlow stood in her bathroom, staring at herself in the mirror, wishing it were February, wishing it were Alaska, wishing she was doing anything but going to a pool party in sweltering Georgia.

Duncan knocked on the door. "Marlow, you ready?"

I cannot do this. Why was she doing this? Why did Duncan feel the need to drag her along to every blasted event Sterling and Alby hosted this week? Was he that desperate for reassurance and security? Did seeing Birdie again make him that upset and nervous? He didn't act like it, acted smooth as butter like always. But he kept insisting Marlow's presence was necessary for his emotional wellbeing. *Like a support pet,* she thought bitterly as she stared at herself in a swimsuit. *Why a pool party? Lord, do you hate me? Am I being punished for something?* She was beginning to wonder. What else was she to think when invited to a pool party with perfect Duncan, Sterling, and Hayden and tiny Alby and Birdie? Marlow was going to look like an Amazon in comparison, and not the Wonder Woman variety. The old school battle-ax depicted in paintings, a longhaired he-man cave dweller.

Duncan knocked again. "Marlow?"

"Marlow's dead now. She left a letter with instructions saying you should go without her."

"I'm coming in," he warned.

"No, wait," she said, but of course he didn't. She lunged for her cover up, but too late. Duncan was in the room and staring at her. "I could have been using the bathroom. You have boundary issues."

"Uh-huh," he agreed, unconcerned. His eyes scanned her from head to toe, literally from the top of her head to the very tips of her red painted toenails. "Same color green as the sofa," he noted, eyes returning to linger speculatively on her swimsuit.

If he says it's the same size as the sofa, too, I will murder him, she thought, but he didn't. Instead he seemed to be waiting for her to comment. Or maybe he was waiting on something else. She couldn't quite read the strange expression now on his face. "My favorite color," she mumbled.

"Really? I thought it would be that same turquoise shade of your eyes."

She squinted. "What kind of conceited freak job matches their favorite color to their own eye shade?" She propped her hand on her hip and regarded him. "Let me guess, your favorite color is dark brown."

"More of a chestnut shade, really," he said, fluttering his lush lashes at her.

Before she could chastise him, he leaned closer and pinched her waist. She twisted away from him. "Did we start playing the game where we touch each other in awkward places and I missed the memo?"

"That was for making us late," he said. Then he leaned in and pressed his lips to her neck, kissing her. "That was because you're pretty and I like you."

She glanced at herself in the mirror, as if for clues. "I'm so confused right now."

"Moral support," he said, tugging her hand to lead her from the bathroom.

"You must have been a particular favorite of the booster club in high school," she said and he laughed.

They arrived at Alby's and greeted everyone. Duncan hauled all of Darla's paraphernalia from the car and began setting it up. "Marlow, how does this contraption go together?" he asked, eyeing a baby flotation device that was seemingly designed by nuclear physicists.

"Those two ends snap in," Marlow called. She sat on a lawn chair with Darla in the shade, still wearing her cover up.

"I tried that. Nearly lost a finger," Duncan said. He was getting annoyed with the blasted thing. She was always better at the mechanics of things than he was. "Can you please come here and do it?"

"Can't you bring it out?" she asked.

"No because it's waterlogged and weighs ten thousand pounds," he said.

"I'm keeping the baby in the shade until it's ready," she said.

"Let's trade places and I'll keep the baby in the shade while you do this. I'm about to curse a blue streak, and Alby won't approve."

Marlow's gaze darted around as if in search of escape.

"What's the matter?" Duncan asked.

She shook her head. He hopped out of the pool and went to sit beside her. "Are you sick?" he asked.

"No."

"Marlow," he prodded.

"I don't necessarily want to get in the pool," she said.

"Can't you swim?"

"I can swim."

"Then why don't you want to get in the pool?" he asked.

"Duncan, do I have to spell it out for you?"

"Apparently," he said.

She sighed. "I don't want to be in my bathing suit in front of all these strangers."

"Why not?" he asked.

She gave him a look. Darla sat between them, playing with her toes. He picked her up and held her so he could scoot closer to Marlow. "First of all, no one here is a stranger."

"Maybe not to you."

"Nobody here is judgy like that," he said.

"I know, but Birdie and Alby are so tiny."

"So? Marlow, come on. This isn't you. Are you your body?"

"No offense, Duncan, but it's a lot easier to take a lecture on body positivity from someone whose body doesn't look like this." She ran a light finger down his impressive abs.

"Who cares about any of that? It's Darla's first time in the water. She might be scared. She needs her Marlow. *I* need my Marlow. Pretty, pretty please? I'll buy you another house, let you renovate it for me." He put his finger under her chin, tipping it toward him.

"I'm doing this for Darla, not because your charm works on me."

"None? Not even a little? Not even the tiniest bit?" He leaned forward, brushing his nose on hers.

"No, I'm immune to your ways," she said, breathless.

"Hmm, too bad." He sat back so abruptly she nearly tumbled off the chair. "Let's get this thing hooked up. I'm sweltering." He adjusted Darla's hat. "Did you already put on her sunscreen?"

"What kind of nanny takes her baby into the Georgia sun without sunscreen?" she returned, easing into the water. She clicked the two pieces together and reached for Darla.

"Thank you for not gloating over how easy you made that seem," Duncan said.

"Oh, I planned to, but I wanted to get the baby settled first," she said.

"Miss Marlow," Hayden Paxton said, emerging from below the water to her left.

Duncan flinched. "Geez, Paxton, are you part turtle?"

"Ha, aquatic humor. Good on you for fully embracing the dad jokes, Shepherd."

"Was there something you particularly wanted to discuss with Marlow?" Duncan asked.

"Yes, in fact there was," Hayden said. Turning to Marlow, he continued, "I hear you are quite the handywoman."

"I do all right," she said modestly.

"She's freaking fantastic," Duncan muttered. "Not that anyone asked my opinion."

"I don't know what your future plans are, but I wanted to say I have a buddy who flips houses and is looking for a partner. Just putting that out there in case, you know, you're unhappy in your current climate or something."

"Unhappy? Why would she be unhappy?" Duncan demanded.

"No reason. It's just that it's all well and good to raise someone else's child, but maybe someday she'll want some of her own. Actually, my buddy's kind of in the market for a wife, too. I'll give him your number." Sensing he had pushed Duncan too far, he dove under the water and swam far away, fast.

"That guy. What is wrong with him? Does he have a biological need to poach the women in my life?"

Marlow tried to stay stoic, but a little giggle escaped before she could tamp it down.

"Do not encourage him," he said, jutting a finger in her face. "In fact, don't even look at him."

"Why would I want to?" she said with feigned innocence. "It's so unappetizing how former firemen keep their bodies in top physical condition, like they're just on standby to run in and save someone. Yuck."

"For your information, no one's ever seen him in uniform. We only have his word for it that he was a fireman. He was probably the volunteer they sent to get donuts for the real fire people."

"Jealousy does not become you, Mr. Shepherd," she said, still fully amused at his expense.

"Then stop giving me reason to be jealous, Miss Spear," he replied.

She squinted at him in confusion. "Me? What are you talking about? I meant," she paused and leaned in, lowering her voice, "Birdie."

"Right, I know. But I don't want him adding any notches to his tally while he's here," Duncan said, pushing Darla in her floatie and pulling her back again.

As if they'd conjured her, Birdie made eye contact and swam over.

"Girl, you are twenty seven years old. Why are you still dog paddling?" Duncan demanded.

"Because I don't want to get my giant head of hair wet," Birdie replied.

"Well, that sounds like a challenge," Duncan said, pushing Darla to Marlow.

"Don't," Birdie said, eyes widening as she began hedging away.

"Come on, now. It's been way too long since I tossed you in the deep end," Duncan said, advancing on her.

"Duncan, do not. Do you understand how long it takes this mess of hair to dry?"

"Do you understand I don't care?"

She tried to get away but wasn't fast enough. Duncan grabbed her and tossed her into the deep end. She rose sputtering. "Duncan Shepherd, you're a menace," she yelled, shooting a stream of water in his direction.

Chuckling, he ducked under the water and swam back to Marlow.

"Way to show her how much you've matured. Good job," Marlow said mildly.

"I can't let everything go. She might have thought I had a terminal illness or something if I didn't throw her in. Tradition and all that." He tipped his head, studying her. "I'd dunk you, if you weren't holding my baby."

She gave him a sweet smile. "Aren't you cute? But the truth is *I'd* dunk *you*, if I weren't holding your baby."

"Birdie, you want to hold the baby a while?" he called, eyes still on Marlow.

"Yes, please," she replied, swimming closer again. "Still hate you," she added, kicking Duncan before she latched onto Darla's floatie.

"Fine, just keep my baby alive," he said, walking through the water, advancing on Marlow. She remained still until he lunged for her, then dodged away, darting under the water.

"Oh, she's got moves," Birdie noted to Darla who was once again busy trying to eat her hair.

After a long game of chase, he eventually caught her. "I should have known you were part fish," he said, breathless.

"We prefer the term mermaid."

"Let me see." He reached for her leg, using it to tug her close and anchor it against him. "Nope, still legs. Long legs, though." He studied her from close up. "You sure are pretty, Miss Marlow Spear."

"Thank you," she said, feeling a little shy and more than a little confused. Was he trying to make Birdie jealous? Must be. Otherwise she didn't understand the new plan.

"You wouldn't actually leave me to flip houses, would you?"

"I don't know," she said slowly. Her hands had nowhere to go. Usually she would grip his shirt to anchor them, but he wasn't wearing one. She could not, would not, put her hands on his bare chest or abs in front of all his friends who could be watching and making judgments. Finally she rested one on the side of the pool and used the other to twirl her own hair.

"What do you mean you don't know?"

"I mean I loved doing your house. I could see me doing something like that."

He frowned. "But…" he glanced at Darla and back to her. "What about us?"

"I'm sure you and Darla would find another nanny, and it's not like I'm quitting today. Certainly not with Chelsea still out of commission."

He frowned harder. "I thought you were happy."

"I am, but this was only ever temporary. You know that, I told you I was trying to get myself sorted and plan a new future, one that doesn't involve teaching."

At some point his hand had shifted to her lower back, pressing her against him. It was more comfortable to rest her hand on his shoulder. His face looked so sad, so forlorn, she opened her mouth to reassure him, to tell him of course she wouldn't leave, when he said four little words that ruined it.

"What about your book?"

CHAPTER 25

Marlow froze. "What?"

Duncan realized his mistake and tried to backpedal. "That is, I mean, um…"

She wriggled free of his embrace and gave him a little shove. "How do you know about my book?"

"I, uh, might have snooped on your laptop, sent a copy to myself, and read it."

She covered her mouth with her hand, gasping. "No."

"But, Marlow, it's good, really good. I read the whole thing in a day. You know how miraculous that is for me. Have you ever seen me read? But I enjoyed your book, really. You creeped me out with that serial killer, and I had no idea how it would end."

"You…you…" she shook her head, edging away from him.

Panicked now, he decided to throw gasoline on the bonfire. "I'm not the only one who thought it was good. Sterling loved it. He thinks you're really talented."

Her jaw dropped lower. She sucked a sharp breath, then closed her mouth and whirled away from him, swimming to the ladder. He followed, trying to pull her back.

"Don't go. Stay and talk to me," he said.

"You want to keep that hand, you'll let me go," she snapped. People were looking at them, but she didn't care. She had never been angrier, never been more mortified.

Duncan likewise realized people were watching him. He dropped his hand, but he followed her up the ladder and out of the pool. "Birdie, you good?" he asked, shooting her an assessing glance.

"We're good here," she said, purposely keeping her eyes on Darla and not the obvious argument taking place as Marlow marched to her chair, wrapped a towel around her body, and stalked away.

Duncan followed.

"Go away," Marlow snapped when he caught up with her.

"You've never been here before. You have no idea where you're going."

He had her there, drat him. She paused and glanced around for escape. "I know a place," he said, turning to head around the corner from the pool. She followed, hoping to at least find a place where no one was looking at her. She rounded the corner and he pulled her into a single stall bathroom. "I used to bring girls here to make out."

She stared at him, blank faced.

"Right, not the time to reminisce, okay." He took a breath. "I'm sorry I snooped in your computer. I thought it was kind of our thing to spy on each other. You read my bank statement."

He had her again, the brat. He was some sort of argument ninja today. "It's not that you spied, it's what you found."

"If you're not mad I spied, explain why you're mad because I don't understand." He took a tentative step closer, "And I want to."

Her cheeks felt like they were on fire. "My writing is really, really personal to me. No one has ever read it before."

"No one?"

She shook her head. "Not Jensen, not even my parents."

"What were you planning to do with it?" he asked, tone gentle.

She twirled the edge of the towel. "I was hoping to find the courage to maybe put it out there. Someday. In the far future. Anonymously."

He took another step closer. "Do you remember when you told me

I had to learn to sing for Sterling's reception? You said I was able to toss a ball in front of hundreds of people, so I should be able to sing in front of the same number. So I'll turn it back on you. You were in pageants. You sang in front of people lots of times. How is writing different than that?"

She swallowed hard, reaching out absently to touch the string on his swim trunks. "I don't know, but it's different somehow. It makes me feel so vulnerable, so exposed."

"But it was so good. And I didn't tell Sterling it was your book. I kept it anonymous, just said I wanted him to read something and give his honest opinion. Honestly, he's been looking at me funny lately. I think he believes I have some latent talent as a writer and is intimidated. Been kind of fun, actually."

She smiled, still looking down. "I'm sorry I overreacted. Kind of a lot, probably. You friends must think I'm insane."

"Uh, Marlow, it's me. If you think watching a woman storm away from me in anger is unusual, you haven't been paying attention."

She wrinkled her nose, finally meeting his gaze. "I don't want them to think I'm one of your regulars, one of your girls."

He took another step closer and touched his finger under her chin, tipping it. "But you are my girl."

"I don't understand what's happening here," she whispered.

"Don't you?" he asked.

"No. Is this some kind of new tactic to make Birdie jealous? To pay attention to me so she'll realize what she's missing?"

His lashes fluttered. "Yes, it's exactly that," he said, tipping forward to brush his lips on hers.

She sucked a breath and pressed her palms to his abs. "How's she going to know about this?"

"Feel free to tell her," he said, kissing her lightly again.

"Seems like a risky plan," she breathed, standing on her toes to try and get closer.

"No, it's foolproof, trust me," he cupped her face, drawing her closer, when someone knocked on the door.

"Hey, um, I'm so sorry to interrupt," Birdie said. "But Darla seemed to realize both of you were out of sight and, um, she's none too happy." Through the door they heard Darla's angry squeal.

"Sorry about that," Duncan said, wrenching the door open. Darla caught sight of Marlow and her squeals morphed to happiness as she lunged. Marlow caught her and pulled her close, kissing her on autopilot. She glanced at Duncan who nudged his head toward Birdie, giving her a look like, *Go ahead, tell her.*

She raised her brows. *Really?*

He gave a definitive nod.

"Um, Birdie."

"Yes?" Birdie said, eyes bright like her avian namesake. She was adorable, all tiny features and big hair. Marlow opened her mouth to tell her about the kiss, but she couldn't, absolutely couldn't, not even for Duncan. It was too odd.

"I love your hair so much," she blurted. *Yeah, that's less odd. Good job, Marlow.* "I always wanted curly hair like that. I have to blow dry mine upside down to get even a hint of volume."

"Oh, thank you," Birdie said, touching the end of one of her curls. "I have to say something to you, too. It's kind of weird, but Duncan can attest to that being my M/O in life."

"True story," Duncan inserted.

"Shut it," Birdie told him, making a closing motion with her hand. To Marlow she added, "I think you are the most beautiful woman I have ever seen in real life. I can say that with authority now because I've seen actual French and Italian women up close. Trying to look directly at you is like trying to watch an eclipse without special glasses." With that, she spun and walked away, leaving Marlow open mouthed behind her.

"Th-thank you," she belatedly called. Birdie tossed a wave but didn't turn around.

"I begin to see the draw between you two. Y'all are odd," Marlow said.

Duncan put his arm around her shoulders and herded her out of the bathroom. "True, and so was everything she said. Like an eclipse without special glasses. I'm going to write that down."

Marlow stared at him. "Odd. So odd."

CHAPTER 26

Marlow flat out refused to go to the rehearsal and dinner with Duncan, just like she'd refused to be there when he showed Birdie the house.

"Why would you want me there?" she'd asked.

"Because you're the one who did it," he had replied, as if it should have been obvious.

"I'm beginning to doubt your reputation as a ladies' man, so let me clue you in: when you're trying to impress a woman with your amazing house, you don't allow another woman to tag along for the ride."

"But Birdie and I are also old friends, and she knows we're good friends. She would expect you to be there," he said.

She stared at him, as she had been doing almost constantly lately, as if he'd taken leave of his senses, which he apparently had. "Are you insane? That makes absolutely no sense. No, I will not accompany you on the house tour and point out all the little touches I've added. She doesn't want to see my contributions, Duncan."

"Of course she does, she likes you," Duncan argued.

At that point she pressed her fingers to her temples and walked away.

They argued again over the rehearsal. "No, absolutely not. There is no reason for me to go to the rehearsal. I'm not in the wedding. No one brings his nanny to his best friend's rehearsal."

"Obviously you wouldn't go as my nanny, you would go as my date," he argued.

"You don't need a date. You're trying to woo the groom's sister. Why am I the only one of us who remembers that? Besides, you won't have time to fraternize with me, you have a lot of best man duties to attend to, a speech, for one."

Duncan had paled slightly at that. "Uh-oh."

"You forgot to write a speech?" Marlow said, tone scathing.

"A lot has been going on," he said. "Besides I still have time."

"It's tonight," she exclaimed.

"But you'll help me, won't you? I mean, you are a writer, aren't you?" He put his arms around her, nuzzling her neck.

"Yes," she dutifully replied. After realizing he'd stolen and read her story, she confessed to writing seven other books. Duncan was making her practice calling herself a writer, to get her more comfortable with the idea. "But you are perfectly capable of writing a charming and witty speech on your own."

"Yes, but with you it will be wittier and more charming," he declared, now nibbling on her earlobe.

"This ear fetish of yours is getting out of hand," she whispered, eyes closed.

"Do you want me to stop?" he whispered, warm breath blowing in her ear.

She shivered. "Soon, probably."

Smiling, he resumed his task.

Now, the day of the wedding, Marlow felt unaccountably nervous. "I'm not the one getting married," she reminded her reflection. She had shopped for a new dress, and she was wearing her body smoothing contraption that went a long way toward sucking in her gut. Her hair was down and curly, mostly because that was how Duncan liked it. When she realized this about herself, she gathered her hair up and reached for a clasp, then dropped it and turned away from the mirror with a huff of disgust. *Dressing for a man. Weak, you are so weak.* On the other hand, she reasoned Duncan would need a fair amount of moral support today. He and Birdie were playing the part of best man and maid of honor. Duncan hadn't said as much, but Marlow felt like it was now or never. What could be more perfect or give the two of them a better chance to catch up?

They'd had a chance the night of the house tour, but all Duncan would tell her was that Birdie had loved the house as much as he thought she would, which was to say a lot.

"Did she cry?" Marlow asked.

"Yes, she did," he affirmed.

"Good cry or bad cry?"

At that he had squinted at her, abashed. "You realize I'm a dude, right? I have no idea how to answer that question, or even why it's a question. Girls are weird."

Marlow loaded Darla and all her accompanying necessities. She loved being a nanny, and loved Darla, but she missed traveling lightly. Gone were the days of grabbing her purse and jetting out the door. Now she needed the overflowing diaper bag, stuffed with anything and everything the baby might need during the long day, up to and including two changes of clothing, multiple diapers, formula, palatable solids, toys, a blanket, and wipes. And still Marlow felt like she was forgetting something. *The kitchen sink, maybe?*

Duncan had been at the church all morning for pictures and to keep Sterling company. Marlow wondered how Alby was holding up and decided to shoot her a text, just in case she had a minute and was feeling anxious.

Good luck today, *future Mrs.! SOOO happy for you! Can't wait for the day to begin.*

The reply came almost immediately, making Marlow wonder if Alby was anxiously sitting on her phone, looking for a way to calm her nerves. *Thank you, Marlow. Sterling and I adore you. I'll be glad to see a friendly face in the crowd!*

MARLOW FELT a little tug on her heartstrings. Alby's parents were dead, she didn't have much family otherwise. Her side would be filled to capacity with people from her company, her charity work. Otherwise she was very much alone, minus Sterling and all his accompanying friends and family. Marlow had the mad desire to divert to her parents' house and spend the day with them in appreciation for their continued presence in her life. It was an impossibility, though. Darla was the flower girl, would ascend the aisle in the arms of Alby's friend, Bess, heavily pregnant with her fourth baby.

She arrived and handed a flouncy Darla over to Bess before finding her seat.

ARE YOU HERE? Duncan texted.

I'M HERE.

COME SEE ME.

IS THAT ALLOWED? she sent, smiling, expectantly awaiting his answer.

GIRL. Get here.

CHUCKLING, she eased from the pew and disappeared behind the platform. Duncan met her in the hallway, stopping short when he caught sight of her.

"I…I…" he began and couldn't seem to get any farther.

"Speechless seems like a good reaction," she said, smoothing her hand self-consciously on her dress.

"I just, I mean…" he waved his hand at her.

She closed the distance between them and tugged his lapels. "You fill out a tuxedo quite nicely, Mr. Shepherd."

"And I you," he sputtered.

She stood on her toes, sniffing his breath. "Are you drunk?"

He rested his forehead on hers. "Yes, but not the way you imagine. Marlow, you…"

"Hey, are you coming?" Sterling poked his head out the door, speaking with unaccustomed nervousness. He caught sight of Marlow and did a double take. "Marlow, my lands, girl. You make that dress come alive."

"Hey," Duncan called. "Eyes on your own paper."

"I bet she made you speak in tongues," Sterling taunted before withdrawing his head back inside the room.

"Ignore him," Duncan said.

"No, it's his day. I should go. Be the best groomsman you can possibly be today for your best friend you love the most of anybody."

"Not the most of anybody, but I get the gist," he said. He kissed her, intending it to be a succinct little brush of affection, but then he had trouble letting go and reached for her, intending to deepen it.

Marlow stepped out of his reach, walking backward away from him. "You go in there now," she directed, pointing at him.

"Turn around so I can watch you walk away," he commanded.

"You're very odd," she said, but she complied, mostly so she wouldn't trip and break an ankle.

He whistled appreciatively. She took out her phone and texted him.

Nice sexism, *boss.*

. . .

Nice...never mind, he replied.

Smiling, she tucked her phone back in her purse.

The ceremony was lovely, and Marlow cried, as she knew she would. Darla made it halfway before she started to fuss. Marlow was about to step in and retrieve her when Duncan crossed the aisle and plucked her from Bess, likely earning the devotion of every female in attendance. Hayden, the second groomsman behind Duncan, winked and smiled at Darla, who eyed him from Duncan's shoulder, laughing in delight at his antics. Duncan turned around, realized what was happening, and shook his head at Hayden in disgust. Marlow had to press her fist to her mouth to bite back her laughter. She thought she was the only one who noticed the exchange, but when she caught sight of Birdie, she was trying hard not to laugh, too.

The ceremony was almost at an end when she felt someone's eyes on her. She turned to Alby's side of the church and caught Hart Wentworth shamelessly staring at her. Forcing herself not to overreact, she gave him a flirtatious little smile and faced forward again. *Hart Wentworth, whoa.* Alby's Atlanta recruit was one of the most eligible men in the state and, if his intense gaze was to be believed, might have just set his sights on Marlow.

Of course he hasn't seen all of me yet, Marlow thought bitterly. She was certain that when he caught the full view, his interest would fritter away. She had never seen an overweight society maven. Either it was against the law in their world or they were shut away out of sight, banished to the place where people with flaws go. When she faced forward again, Duncan caught her eye. His expression made it clear he had caught the exchange with Hart. He shook his head and mouthed, *No,* and she almost laughed out loud again.

On his way down the aisle, Duncan handed Darla to Marlow. By this time she had grown sleepy and immediately cuddled up and fell asleep in Marlow's grasp, which was sweet but made carrying her purse and diaper bag impossible.

"May I help you?" Marlow knew without looking the voice

belonged to Hart Wentworth. What was more, it wasn't a chance encounter. He would have had to cross the aisle on purpose to get to her.

"Thank you, that would be lovely," Marlow said sincerely. She needed a couple more hands today, and he was willing to provide them. She smiled. He blinked at her, reminding her of her earlier meeting with Duncan. What was it with the men of the world today?

"I don't believe we've had the pleasure," he said. "You're Duncan Shepherd's nanny, is that right?"

"Yes, sir, Marlow Spear. And I'm so sorry, but I didn't catch your name."

He blinked at her again. Absolutely every woman in Georgia under the age of forty knew who Hart Wentworth was, whether she was single or not. He was that sought after, that handsome and debonair. Marlow knew too, of course, but this wasn't her first fall off the turnip truck. Men like Hart always enjoyed a challenge.

"My name is Hart Wentworth."

"Oh, what a nice name. Mr. Wentworth, I'm rather new to the area, up from Savannah. Are you from here?"

"Please call me Hart, I don't think I'm old enough to be Mr. Wentworth to you."

"Maybe I'm that young, Hart," she interjected.

He smiled. "I guess it will have to remain a mystery. I wouldn't venture to guess a lady's age."

"Better to guess her age than whether or not she's a lady," she replied, and he laughed. "But to set your mind at ease about legality, I'm recently twenty six."

"Now why would I mind if you're legal or not?"

"Liquor license. You look like the kind that might try to ply a girl with alcohol." She tipped her head, studying him askance as if he were suspicious.

"My daddy always said if you have to get a girl drunk, you're doing it wrong."

"Strange words from a father," she said.

"Strange father," he replied, and she laughed. "Didn't your dad ever toss you any pearls of wisdom?"

"Yes, but they all came from the bible. My daddy's a Baptist preacher."

He winced. "All the women in the world, and I have to find a preacher's daughter."

"Maybe I'm the only woman left you haven't gone out with yet," she suggested.

He laughed. "I thought you didn't know who I was."

"You're a man, aren't you? I know you're type."

"Oh, no, Miss Marlow. Please don't tell me you're embittered."

"My goodness gracious, no sir. I don't think people turn bitter until they get to be your age," she said, smiling sweetly.

"You're a southern girl, through and through," he said, shaking his head slowly.

"Thank you," she said.

"I'm not certain it was a compliment," he replied.

"Take it as a warning," she said and eased away from him to her table. She was suddenly glad for assigned seating. Flirting with Hart was fun, but something was lacking, and she didn't know what. Or maybe it was the fact that she had a very heavy, very sleeping baby in her arms. To be fully on her game, she would need to be Darla-free. *Hart still has my purse and diaper bag.* She wondered why he hadn't brought them to her table and realized it was a power play on his part. *He wants me to come to him.* She appreciated his strategy, but she didn't have much heart for the game today.

"Hi, sweetie." She was assigned to a table with Duncan's parents and grandparents. She had met them on numerous occasions and loved them all, almost as if they were her family and not his.

"Hi," she replied in a whisper, not wanting to startle Darla.

"Aw, the little angel plum conked out," Grammy said. Grammy was Duncan's grandmother, the original owner of the farm. Marlow had been nervous to reveal the renovation to her, but she had cried—happy tears, Marlow made certain. *It's all the things I wanted to do but never could,* she'd said. None of the family had ever had Duncan's level of income. She wondered if that was one more reason he bought the family farmstead, to provide his grandparents some measure of financial stability in their waning years.

Probably, because he's secretly sweet that way, she thought.

Her phone buzzed with a text. She didn't realize she still clutched it in her hand until she felt it buzz. *Why you looking all dreamy? Better not be Hart Wentworth. Guy's a player.*

TAKES ONE TO KNOW ONE, *I guess,* she replied one handed.

IF YOU WEREN'T HOLDING *my baby...* He threatened.

YOU'D WHAT?

I'LL SHOW YOU LATER, he replied. Cheeks flushed, she set down her phone.

CHAPTER 27

"*D*o you want us to feed you?" Grammy offered as Marlow ate one handed.

"Thank you, ma'am, but I've grown used to doing things with one hand," Marlow replied, smiling.

"You're so competent," Grammy said, patting Marlow's shoulder. "And, my lands, about the prettiest face I've ever seen."

Marlow tried not to wince. There it was, the pretty face comment, sneaked in just as she was feeling a high after her flirty conversation with Hart. "Thank you, ma'am," Marlow said, hoping she sounded sincere, rather than forced.

Darla woke and whimpered to be fed. Her food was in her bag, the bag currently in Hart's possession. Marlow sighed. There was nothing for it but to drop her pride and retrieve the bag. But before she could get up, the bag and her purse dropped into her lap, deposited by Duncan who stood frowning beside her.

"I noticed Hart Wentworth still had these in his possession and thought I'd retrieve them for you, thereby saving you the torture of being once again subjected to his stupid face."

"Why, thank you, Mr. Shepherd. You are ever so helpful and kind," Marlow said.

"Hart Wentworth?" Grammy piped up. "Oh, my lands, that boy is a fine specimen. Was he talking to our Marlow?"

Marlow sputtered a laugh. Duncan scowled first at her, then at his grandmother. "Pardon me, Grammy, but she is not *our* Marlow, she is *my* Marlow, and she has no call to be talking to Hart Wentworth. I've played basketball with him a few times. Let me tell you, he is not the gentleman y'all seem to believe he is."

"He plays basketball?" Marlow said, perking up.

"Not with you, he doesn't," Duncan said. "Although maybe I should let him. Ego like that, you'd crush his dreams and his spirit and he'd never bother with you again."

"That might be the sweetest thing you've ever said to me."

He leaned close to whisper in her ear. "Plenty more where that came from. Do you need anything? Want me to take a turn with the baby?"

"I'm fine," she replied.

"Too true," he said, kissing her cheek before heading back to the head table. She watched him go with a smile. When she faced forward, all of his family was beaming at her.

"Well," Grammy said, wriggling excitedly. Beside her, her daughter, Sue, wriggled in the same fashion. Marlow broke out in a panic sweat.

"If y'all will excuse me, I'm going to change Darla out of her fancy dress so she can eat." She walked away from the table, trying not to sprint as if fleeing an attacker. What was Duncan doing putting ideas in his family's head about them? She got that none of his family knew he had feelings for Birdie. Making them think he had feelings for her seemed a far way to go to throw them off track. Unless…but no. He had already made it clear her body precluded any lasting attraction to her. Perhaps Birdie's arrival had sent him into some downward spiral of neediness and longing. She would try to be nicer to him to make up for the deficit.

She gave Darla a piece of wheat toast to gnaw while she changed her. Duncan was predictably strict about the baby's diet, not wanting her to have sugar or processed foods. But Marlow always sneaked some butter on her toast. It was their little secret, and Darla seemed to thank her for it, lunging for the toast with glee whenever it was in sight.

"We girls have to stick together," she told Darla who ignored her completely in favor of her food. "I see so much of myself in you," she added, picking her up to kiss her cheeks.

When she exited the bathroom, she ran into Hart Wentworth who made no secret of the fact that he was waiting there for her. "How old is the baby?" he asked, smiling at her. Everyone smiled at Darla. She was that adorable.

"Nine months."

"She's a beauty. Are you certain she's not yours?"

She tipped her head at him. "Are you accusing me of having a secret baby out of wedlock and trying to pass it off as charm?"

He squinted. "It sounded a lot smoother in my head."

She laughed. "Don't take it too hard. We all have off days. Keep practicing on other girls and get back to me when you have it perfected."

"Hmm," Hart said, studying her as if not certain if she was uninterested or just good at keeping him on his toes. At this point she wasn't certain either. It was Hart Wentworth; she'd be insane not to at least consider him. Wouldn't she?

She returned to the table and her phone buzzed with a text from Duncan.

Does he have a tracker on you?

Do you? she returned.

You have my heart. It's vital I track your whereabouts.

. . .

SHE GLANCED down at Darla and kissed the top of her head. *She's doing fine,* she assured him.

??? HE SENT IN RETURN, and she had no idea what that meant.

She spent the next little bit helping Darla demolish a shocking amount of food. Where did she put it? *Oh, to have the metabolism of a baby,* she thought. Then again, if all she got to eat was avocados, wheat toast, and sweet potatoes, she might go to town on them without remorse, too.

When Darla was finished eating, it was necessary to take her back to the bathroom and clean her. Once again, Hart was there when she left, leaning against the wall.

"I know why you look so familiar," he said.

"You do?" she returned, heart sinking. She had hoped he wouldn't remember.

"Yes, you were in the Miss Georgia pageant a few years back. I was one of the judges."

"Oh," she drawled as if it were new information, though she had known all along.

"For what it's worth, I voted you the highest. I thought you had it in the bag," he said.

"I had nothing on the girl with the three legged dog. A good sob story gets them every time," she said.

"Not me. I remained stone cold and in your favor," he said, holding up his hand as if taking an oath.

"Hart Wentworth," Duncan said, inserting himself into the conversation.

"Duncan," Hart said, giving him a nod. "I was just admiring your, uh, baby." He indicated Marlow with a flourish.

"Isn't she spectacular," Duncan said. "You should go back to Atlanta and get one of your own."

"Oh, my," Marlow said.

"Marlow and I were reminiscing over old times," Hart said.

"Really? She's never mentioned you to me. Ever," Duncan said, taking a sip of his drink.

"That's because she didn't know me then, but I knew her," Hart said.

"Hart was apparently one of the judges from my failed pageant bid," Marlow said. "The memories are so pleasant."

Duncan snickered. He knew she didn't enjoy rehashing the pageants.

"I should go give my congratulations to Alby and Sterling," Hart said. "I'm here about half the week, so maybe we'll bump into each other on some other occasion."

"It's a small town," Marlow said smiling, noncommittal.

"Bye bye then," Duncan said, eyes narrowed as Hart headed away. "Does no one respect territory anymore?"

"What on earth has gotten into you today?" Marlow demanded. "Why are you acting all possessive and jealous? And what was that little display in front of your family?"

He stared at her, his mouth opening and closing a few times until they were interrupted by his parents.

"Marlow," his mother said.

"Fredandsue," she greeted them. Duncan did a double take at her.

"We wondered if Darla might want a bit of Gammy and Pap time," Sue said.

"I think you're in luck, Mama. She was just asking when you guys were going to take her," Duncan said.

His mother squinted at him in confusion. "She talks now?"

"I was joking, Mama. But she has been saying some words, mostly Dada and Mama."

"Oh," Sue squealed, clasping her hands together in delight. "Try to get it on film for me. And Chelsea must be thrilled."

"Well, since Darla's been spending so much time with us, she's been saying it to Marlow. We've been keeping it on the down low until Chelsea recovers," Duncan said. "Don't want to make her feel bad."

"I don't think she's saying Mama," Marlow interjected. "I think she's trying to say Marlow."

"No, baby, she's saying Mama," Duncan contradicted.

"Well anyway, we wondered if we might borrow Darla a bit and make the rounds. We have to introduce our angel to some long lost friends and relations," Sue said.

"Why yes, ma'am, of course. You come and find me when you're ready to give her back," Marlow said, handing Darla over.

"Why'd you say it like that?" Duncan asked after they disappeared with the baby.

"I *do* think she's trying to say Marlow. It's the way she says it, different from Mama, like she's reaching for the R," Marlow said.

"Not that, my parents' names. Why'd you say them all jumbled up like that, like a sneeze?" he asked.

"That's how they say their names. Haven't you ever noticed? They say them all bunched up in a pile."

"No, they don't," he said, smiling.

She nodded. "I'll prove it, look. Your mom has her sights set on Sterling's cousin Taylor's date. Listen in as she introduces them. Be sneaky."

"Girl, I don't know any other way," he said. He took her hand and they edged closer to his parents as they made their approach to Taylor and his date, leaning in in time to hear Sue say, "Fredandsue."

Duncan pressed his hand over his mouth and backstepped them away. "Oh, man, why'd you do that? Now I can never unhear it."

"Sorry," Marlow said. They were standing very close together, his arm around her waist, her face tipped and smiling. Suddenly it was as if the air was sucked from the room. Marlow didn't understand why it kept happening that way lately. Everything was in a muddle, and she began to feel confused.

"What's that frowny face for?" he asked, sliding his finger along her nose.

"Nothing," she said, unsure how to broach the topic without drawing attention to it. Maybe not knowing was better.

He leaned closer to whisper in her ear. "Did I mention how incredibly gorgeous and amazing you are?"

"No, but I don't think you're supposed to say things like that about another woman at someone's wedding," she said.

"I wasn't just talking about today. But my lands, girl, you in that dress. Bout gave me a heart attack."

"You covered it well," she said, patting his chest.

He chuckled. "You shocked me speechless and gave me a stutter."

She nestled closer, resting her head on his shoulder, feeling her own sudden need to cling. She had a premonition that everything was about to change, and maybe not for the better. Something felt like it was spiraling toward a collision, and maybe *that* was the explanation for Duncan's strange behavior. Maybe he realized things couldn't go on as they had been, now that Birdie was home.

Sterling and Alby took their first dance and more people began to ease out onto the dance floor.

"Are you going to go ask Birdie to dance?" That was what it had all been about, after all.

"I think I need a refresher from my teacher," he said, taking her hand and leading her onto the dance floor. He pulled her close, snuggling her against him as they started to sway.

"This is not what I taught you," she said, but she wasn't complaining. It was nice, the closeness, the warmth, the belonging.

"I'm waiting for my moment," he said, bestowing his blazing smile on her. The music switched to a more upbeat song and, true to his word, he started to dance, to *really* dance, the way she'd taught him. Alby and Sterling were both good dancers, and so was Hart Wentworth and whoever he was dancing with, so they weren't a spectacle as they cut loose and showed off his new skills.

Breathless after a few songs, they eased off the floor to retrieve a drink. That was when Birdie and Hayden found them.

"Someone taught Duncan to dance," Birdie said. "Color me amazed. No more hip gyrations."

"My hip gyrations wooed many a female heart," Duncan defended.

Birdie pretended to gag. Marlow nudged Duncan who gave her a little nod and stepped forward, extending his hand. "Would you care to take a turn, Miss Birdie Thompson, if that is your real name?"

Birdie flushed and, with a little nod, put her hand in his.

"What did that mean?" Marlow asked Hayden.

"Who can know? They have quite the history," he replied, eyeing her. "How about it, Miss Marlow? Would you like to take a turn on the dance floor?"

"Why, Hayden Paxton, I'd be delighted," she said, putting her hand in his with a little curtsy.

"How does it feel to be home?" she asked as they started to dance to a slow song.

"Honestly? Kind of weird. I didn't know when I went away I would end up loving it so much. I mean, I knew I loved Birdie, and that was why I went. But I love being on the ocean, being overseas. It's a whole different life, one I never envisioned. Strange how that can happen, isn't it? How surprising life can be. And now I've blurted out my life story. Aren't you glad you asked?"

She laughed. "Yes, in fact I am. I regret I haven't gotten to know you as well as I would have liked. It's been such a blur with the wedding and the reno and having Darla full time. And now I'm the one who's blurting. Sorry."

"No, I like it, this is good stuff, good insights. Tell me more, start with Duncan." He wagged his brows at her.

"What's to tell? I work for him, we're friends."

"And you live together and spend every waking moment together and look at each other like…" he trailed off.

"Like what?" she asked with sincere curiosity. What did other people see when they were together?

"Let's just say if I were still a fireman, I'd be following you two around with a hose. And for personal reasons, I'm ever so thankful for your presence." They turned to look at Duncan and Birdie together, talking and laughing as they twirled.

"Is it hard to see her with him?" she asked.

"Yes, but not because I don't trust Birdie. My first wife cheated on me and sometimes I get a twinge, a memory of that wound.

Some pain goes so deep you wonder if you'll ever get over it, you know?"

"I do," she agreed, nodding. It was that way with her weight, all the little insults and comments that sunk down to her soul and lingered. She couldn't meet anyone now without that between them, the suspicion that they saw her as less because she was overweight. "It's very tiresome."

"It is. The good news is that when you find a person, your person, he or she helps you get over it. Love is a miraculous tonic." He darted another smiling glance at Birdie.

"Look at you, looking at her. What a lucky lady is Miss Birdie Thompson."

"And what a lucky fella is Mr. Duncan Shepherd."

"I don't think…" she began, but he cut her off.

"I've known Duncan all my life. You can guess I'm not his biggest fan, for several reasons. But even I don't think he's stupid enough to let the best thing that's ever happened to him go."

"My lands, I'm blushing something fierce," she said.

He smiled. "You are. It's charming."

"What did Sterling and Alby tell you about me?"

"They said we had to meet this Marlow girl, that Duncan acts like a new creation when he's with her. And it's true. And we are all in your debt."

"Ahem, the song is over," Duncan said. He and Birdie stood beside them, hand in hand. But he passed Birdie off to Hayden and took Marlow instead, leading her away.

"Man, that guy," he said.

"Is a sweetheart," Marlow said, mostly to annoy him, but also because it was true. She no longer had the heart to try and affect a coup, to ease Hayden away and Duncan into his spot. Hayden and Birdie were not unhappy; they were solid. How would that realization affect Duncan? Or had it already and that was the cause of his newfound devotion to her? "But you're sweeter," she added, slipping her arm around him to give him a side hug.

"A minority opinion," he said, easing his arm around her shoulders and returning the hug.

"That's because nobody knows you like I do," she said, and it was true. Duncan was generous, incredibly hardworking, kind in small, thoughtful ways. Nobody saw all the little things he did for his family and others because he didn't tell them about it. But Marlow saw, Marlow knew.

He gave her a squeeze. "It's time to go make my toast. Are you going to save me a dance or two after?"

"I'll consider it, but only because it would be awkward to offend my boss," she said.

"Remind me to punish you later for your backtalk," he said, and then he tipped her face and kissed her, at the edge of the dance floor, in front of God and everybody, leaving Marlow staring into space, shocked and flustered.

And then, before she could fully recover, Duncan gave his toast.

"I met Sterling the first day of t-ball when we were five years old. Maybe some guiding star told me to hitch my wagon to his, or maybe I was a lonely kid in search of a brother. Whatever the reason, I count it as one of the luckiest days, to have met and formed a bond with someone who has always been there for me, even when I didn't deserve it, even when I did my best to mess it up. I'm honored to be Sterling's best man today, but it's a misnomer because everyone who knows us understands Sterling is the better man, the best man. And I couldn't think of anyone more deserving of him than his sweet Alby, whom I also love so much. Marlow convinced me to sing a song in their honor today, and I honestly don't know if that's a punishment to me or to them, but I am learning that sometimes music says more from the heart than we could ever say with our words. So, to the happy couple. Please forgive me for what's about to take place."

He set aside the microphone and reached for Marlow's guitar. There was a special kind of hush in the room, expectant, anxious. Most people who knew Sterling also knew Duncan, the two had been a pair since early days. No one in the room had ever heard him sing before, never even knew he had an inclination. Suddenly Marlow felt a burst of nerves on his behalf. What had she been thinking, setting him up this way? He'd never played or sang in front of an audience in his life, and she thought the time to debut a solo was at his best friend's wedding reception? The plan had seemed so clear in the beginning: sing a song, woo Birdie. But it was apparent the plan wouldn't work, and now Duncan was stuck singing in front of everyone for no reason.

She wondered if he was thinking the same because he didn't look at Birdie once through the song, even though it was about finding life-long love with a best friend. He kept his eyes trained on Marlow, so much that other people started to look at Marlow—Sterling, Alby, Birdie, Hayden, all of Duncan's kin at her table.

Her cheeks were flushed—with embarrassment, but also with pleasure. Duncan performed as well as he did everything else, which was to say he was amazing. If she put him and Jensen side by side, no one would know Jensen had been performing forever and this was Duncan's first time.

The song ended and it was time for Birdie's toast, but Marlow didn't hear a word of it. Instead she reached for her phone, intending to send Duncan a congratulatory text but words failed her. In the end, that was what she came up with.

THAT WAS...*I'M without words.*

NOW YOU KNOW *how I felt when you walked into that hallway today.*

SHE SHOOK HER HEAD. There was no comparison between the two. Looking nice all dressed up was completely different than putting yourself out there and being brave. That thought forced her to come up with more words.

. . .

No, that was amazing. YOU are amazing. I am SO, SO proud of you, of the man you're becoming, the man you are. You make me believe again. She thought Jensen had irrevocably broken that part of her, made her cynical and distrusting. But now, an impossibly short time later, Duncan of all people was showing her the opposite was true. There were still good men in the world, and she counted one of them as her very best friend.

THAT'S all I could ever want, he replied.

MARLOW HAD REMAINED stoic through his speech, kept dry eyes through his song, but those six words were her undoing. Pressing her lips together, she turned her head from his view and cried into her napkin.

CHAPTER 28

The toasts ended, but Duncan's best man duties didn't. He was busy and attentive for a while as Marlow composed herself, repaired her face, and made the rounds, dancing once with Sterling's cousin, Taylor, and twice with Hart Wentworth. He tried to flirt, and maybe she returned it, but her mind was in a bit of a daze. Everything felt different today. She couldn't articulate why, but her heart was beating fast, her palms sweaty every time she caught sight of Duncan.

Duncan, meanwhile, tried hard to be present and attentive for Sterling, but it was a struggle. His mind was on Marlow. She seemed so distracted. Was it somehow possible she didn't know, didn't understand what was going on? She was smart, sharp, and confident. But she seemed so flustered every time he touched her that it was making him doubt himself.

"How's it going with Marlow?" Sterling asked as they stood at the edge of the dance floor. Alby was taking a turn with Hart Wentworth and Marlow was somewhere about, making the rounds, he supposed. He'd track her down in a minute, dance with her again. The need to touch her, to reassure himself of her proximity, was almost overwhelming.

"I don't know. I know her better than anybody, present company excluded, but I can't read her on this," Duncan said, his frustration palpable.

"The signs look good from the outside," Sterling said.

Duncan shrugged, ready to talk about something else. He got it now, what Sterling used to tell him about his relationship with Alby. It felt too tender, too special to share with anyone else, even a lifelong best friend. "Fair warning, Grammy is looking to unload her giant old cat on you. I get the feeling she's going to try to cloak it as a wedding gift you can't refuse."

"That old cat is still alive? The huge one?"

"Yes, and she's gotten bigger."

Unseen by them, Marlow appeared behind them, hovering, wanting to speak with Duncan but not wanting to interrupt. And there was maybe a secret small part of her that hoped she might hear something about herself.

"She is so fat," Duncan continued unaware. "I mean, the Titanic has nothing on her. Practically takes a lever to pry her off the couch."

"Oh, no," Sterling said, shaking his head, pressing his hands to his ears. But Duncan was just getting warmed up.

"I'm serious here. She sat on my hand once, it went numb in four seconds."

"Stop it," Sterling said, but he was laughing, they were both laughing. Marlow eased away, pain knifing through her chest, unable to believe the way they'd just been talking about her. Duncan, still unaware of her arrival or departure, continued.

"I'm just trying to be up front with you, because you're my best friend. Otherwise I'd be glad for Grammy to get rid of the thing. She has one wonky eye and diabetes."

Sterling clutched his stomach. "My lands."

"I ought to kidnap it, take it to a vet, and put it down. Get it out of everyone's misery."

"Why don't you?" Sterling asked.

"Marlow," they said together.

"She's tender about those kinds of things. Might never forgive me if I killed Grammy's cat." The conversation paused as they both watched Hart Wentworth twirl Alby on the dance floor, talking and laughing. "I kind of hate that guy."

"Me too," Sterling agreed. "But I'll say this about him: He respects boundaries. Might be time to set some, if you catch my drift."

"Something to ponder," Duncan said. He turned and scanned the crowd. Where was Marlow?

Somehow they never met up the rest of the evening, until it was time to go home. "I'm glad you dropped me off this morning so I can take you home," Duncan said. "There's something extra special about going home with the prettiest girl at the party." He shot her a smile, but her head was turned to the window. "Something wrong?"

"Why would anything be wrong?" she asked, still without looking at him.

"I don't know, but you seem a bit out of sorts. Are you sick?"

"No, I'm fine, thank you."

Duncan gripped the steering wheel. It was definitely the kind of fine that wasn't fine. "I can't fix it if I don't know the problem."

No response.

He let out a breath. "How about I'll put Darla to bed and we'll meet back up on the couch, discuss the day's events."

"She needs a bath," Marlow said vaguely.

He tamped down his annoyance. Something about her affect was off, and he wished she would tell him instead of making him guess. She wasn't normally like that, and the fact that she was now made him think it was something dreadful.

"Did Hart say something to you?" he asked, a ridiculous amount of hope in his tone. It would solve a lot of his problems if the guy had been a jerk.

"No, he's very charming."

"If you like that sort," he said sourly.

No response.

"Marlow, what is wrong with you?"

"Tired, I guess. Long day."

It was more than that, he knew, but he wasn't getting anywhere by pressing her. "I'll be on the couch after I bathe and put Darla to bed. Why don't you come find me when you're ready to talk?"

She didn't reply, but he had confidence she would seek him out. She was much too reasonable to stay mad over nothing. But when he woke on the couch a few hours later, he realized she never showed up. He went upstairs and paused outside her door, hand raised, ready to knock and barge in. But maybe that wasn't the best thing. He had never known Marlow to withdraw like this. Maybe what she actually needed was space for once. In the morning, he was certain they'd get it all sorted out.

Several hours later, he woke to Darla crying. Technically the weekend was Marlow's time off, but she was an early riser and sometimes got Darla first, if she heard her fuss. Maybe she really was tired and slept in today, Duncan thought as he stumbled to the baby's room and picked her up. He gathered her close, soothing her as he bounced, and went next door to Marlow's room, pausing to listen, but there was only silence within. He turned the handle, pushed open the door, and stopped short. No Marlow. Her bed was empty and crisply made. It was unlike her to be awake and not retrieve Darla, mostly because she couldn't stand to hear her cry.

He went downstairs calling her name, but it was obvious the house was empty.

"Marlow," he tried, poking his head in the garage. Her car was gone. With a sudden feeling of foreboding, he dodged back upstairs and opened her closet. *Empty.*

"Nope," he said out loud and returned downstairs. He buckled Darla in her seat, stuck her in the car, and started to drive. He wasn't cognizant of where he was going, exactly, but there weren't a lot of options. Marlow spent all her time with him and his friends. She wouldn't go to any of them. That left only one place.

He parked in her parents' driveway, retrieved Darla, marched up the walk, and banged on the door. Her father opened it, blinking in question at Duncan.

"Good morning, Reverend Spear. I'm sorry to bother you, but I need your daughter."

"Uh," Marlow's dad said, torn between polite manners and loyalty to his daughter. Duncan peered around him, poking his head inside, and caught sight of Marlow in the background, frozen like a deer in headlights, a bowl of cereal in her hands. Caught, she set down the bowl of cereal, opened the back door, and sprinted outside.

"Stop!" Duncan yelled. He set Darla's carrier on the step and took off after her.

Reverend Spear picked up Darla's carrier and set it by the back picture window, watching the action. "What's going on?" his wife asked, joining him.

"Marlow just hopped the fence. Duncan cleared it, too," he said.

"Think he'll catch her?"

"I'd say the odds are pretty even at this point. Wish we could see how it turns out."

"Something tells me we'll know," his wife said. She glanced down and noticed Darla. "Oh good, they left the baby." She bent and unbuckled her, pulling her out and gathering her close. "Let's practice some more, Darla. Can you say 'Grandma, *Grand-ma*'?"

Meanwhile Duncan was gaining on Marlow. She had almost lost him at the fence; she was better at hurdles. But he was faster and she was barefoot. Plus he was fueled by rage. She only had panic on her side.

Eventually he reached out and grasped the back of her shirt, jerking her to a halt. She rounded on him, fighting like a wet cat, and yanked free. He lunged, tackling her to the ground where they wrestled back and forth. By now he'd learned how she fought, and also how to defeat her, though she didn't make it easy. Finally he pinned her. Panting, they stared at each other a few beats, trying to catch their breath.

"What on earth do you think you're doing, running away like that?" he asked.

"I can't work for you anymore," she said.

"Why not?"

"You know why."

"If I knew why, do you think I'd have chased you across the country-side in the clothes I slept in?" he asked.

She pressed her lips together.

"Talk," he demanded.

"I heard you."

"I should hope so, I'm two inches from your face," he snapped.

"I heard you last night, heard what you said to Sterling."

He searched his memory for whatever stupid, insensitive thing he might have uttered. It wasn't beyond the realm of possibility, but try as he might, he couldn't think of a thing. "What did I say?"

"I don't want to repeat it," she said, tears springing to her eyes.

He gasped, pained. "Marlow, please. I really have no idea. Please tell me."

"You said...you said I was so fat I needed a lever to get me off the couch, that I sat on your hand and it went numb." Tears leaked out her eyes and rolled down her cheeks, but he couldn't help it; he sputtered a laugh. Of course it was the wrong thing, and she began to fight him again.

"I was talking about the cat," he yelled.

She froze. "Cat? What cat?"

"Grammy's cat."

"Lady Pawpaw?"

"Yes. She was planning to try and pawn her off on Sterling. I was warning him."

"Oh," Marlow said, cheeks flushing, embarrassed at her overreaction. "Oops. Sorry."

"I don't believe you," Duncan said, annoyed. "I would never say something like that about you, and even if you thought I did, why would you not..." he trailed off, blinking at her.

"What?" she whispered.

His face spread into a slow smile. "You love me."

"How did you get that from *this*?" she asked, wriggling.

"Because every other time I've ever said something rude or stupid or insulting, and let's be honest that's been a lot, you've come at me like a stuck bull, finger in my face, telling me to get my act together.

Never once have you run away and hidden. There could only be one reason for the sudden change. You love me, and it hurt too much to face me."

"You don't know what you're talking about," she said, but she wouldn't make eye contact.

"Look me in the eye and tell me you don't love me," he commanded.

She forced her eyes to his and opened her mouth, but the words wouldn't come. The tears did, though. "Why are you doing this to me?" she whispered.

"Don't cry," he whispered.

"I can't believe you're taking pleasure in my humiliation," she sniffled.

"Humiliation? What are you talking about? Why would it be humiliating to love someone?"

"When they don't love you back, it's pretty degrading," she snapped.

He laughed, the wrong thing again. Her fighting was renewed. He put all his weight on her, pressing her into the ground. "Oh, Marlow. What you don't know could fill a stadium, you know that?"

"What are you talking about?" she asked.

"Do you honestly think I would be here with my hair uncombed in my pajamas in the middle of the street for anything less than abject devotion? Do you not understand how conceited I am about my appearance?"

"You are that," she agreed. "But what about Birdie?"

"She's married," he said.

She blinked, shocked. "What?"

"She and Hayden got married a few months ago and have been keeping it secret. I knew the second she stepped off the plane. Girl never could keep anything off her face. I finally got her to admit it last night. They're thinking of buying a house in Italy. She's been working up the nerve to tell Sterling and her mom."

"Birdie's married?"

He nodded.

"I'm so sorry." She shook her hands free and smoothed them on his face, cupping his cheeks.

"Why? I'm not. No, that's not true. I was. My ego stung for a second at the rejection, but it went away."

"But you love her," Marlow said, confused all over again.

"I did. I loved her in a first love kind of way, with full emotion. But it was a selfish kind of love, all about me and my needs and my wants and my wishes. It was never about Birdie or what she wanted or what was best for her. She tried to tell me before she went away, but I didn't understand. I didn't get it until someone came along and showed me what unselfish love looked like, and the profound effect it can have on a person."

"Uh, are you talking about me now?" she asked uncertainly.

He smiled. "Yes, Marlow. I am talking about you. *You* made me want to be a better man, *you* made me grow up, not Birdie. You with your willingness to take me on and not back down, to tell me all the hard truths I needed to hear while still taking care of me the best. You with your impossible mix of strength and softness. I'll always love her in a way, like family, will always have a spot in my heart for that girl I've known forever. But it's not the biggest place, not the most important part. Not the part that makes me want to spend the rest of my life with a person, the part that makes me live and die based on her happiness. That part is for you, only ever for you." He smoothed his thumb over her bottom lip, staring at it.

"But you're not attracted to me that way."

"Who said?" he asked, eyes snapping to hers.

"*You* said, many times," she replied, frustrated.

"That was the old Duncan. He's dead now. The new Duncan is fully on board with all of this." His hand eased up and down her body, pausing to give her waist a pinch.

"Color me cynical, but I'm afraid I'm going to need more convincing of your miraculous change of heart," she said.

"You're kind of a pain sometimes, you know that? But okay. It started that night you and Jensen broke up, when I held you in my arms and never wanted it to end. I swear it was like I underwent some sort of crucible that night, a baptism by fire, and by the time it was over, I was in love with you. You're so unbreakable, so right for me in all the ways. Do you know what I would do to a lesser girl? I'd crush her. Not on purpose, but the outcome would be the same. But you, you give as good as I do." He paused, staring hard at her face, fighting a smile. His hand brushed the hair at her temple. "I couldn't stop finding ways to try and get my hands and lips on you again, kind of pathetic actually. I don't think I've been that desperate to touch a girl since…No, I don't think I've ever been that desperate to touch a girl, and it was torture because you were *right there.* But you have a good poker face, so I honestly didn't know if you were feeling the same. And you kept shoving me at Birdie. Why did you keep shoving me at Birdie?"

She rolled her eyes. "Because it was what you wanted."

"It was what I *wanted*, not what I *want*. Let me tell you what I want, so we're clear. I want you at the end of every day, at the end of every road, in every possible way, forever. I've wanted it so long I'm sick with it, and you kept dodging me. Why are you so good at dodging me?" He scowled.

"Because I thought you were repulsed by me, based on words that formerly came out of your mouth on multiple occasions." She was nearly torn in half by adulation and exasperation. His words had the effect of making her want to swoon or punch him. Probably both.

"I guess I fell in love with you in phases, first with your face, then with your heart. And then I fell in love with your body. Every delightful, voluptuous inch of it."

"For real?" she asked, still skeptical.

"If you could peek inside my daydreams, you would not have doubts. That day a couple of weeks ago, the day of the pool party, when I opened the door and saw you in your sexy little swimsuit, it was all I could do not to peel you like a grape leaf."

"A grape leaf?" she asked, grimacing.

"It was the first green thing that came to mind. The point is I am a devoted fan of your curves. I can no longer look at an hourglass without getting a little weak-kneed. Why do you think I was hustling so hard to get you out of the house? I had about ten seconds of willpower left in me. It's about all I've had since, too." He tried to kiss her but she dodged him.

"So that's it, then. Just like that you think I'm going to drop everything and roll over in delight. After *months* of stinging rejection and body shaming, I'm supposed to be elated that you've changed your mind about me?"

"Yes?" he tried.

She smiled. "Okay. I should probably cancel my date with Hart Wentworth, though."

"Why don't you let me do that," he suggested.

"Because you won't be able to without using your fists," she said.

"Baby, you know me so well," he murmured, lips now moving against hers.

"And yet I love you anyway."

"Hallelujah," he muttered and kissed her again.

Thank you for reading *Darling Duncan,* the third book in the Georgia Peaches Trilogy. For more books, please check out my website www.-vanessagraybartal.com

www.ingramcontent.com/pod-product-compliance
Lightning Source LLC
Chambersburg PA
CBHW021147190726

48288CB00008B/2856